Samuel French Acting Edition

CW00505311

Lebensraum

by Israel Horovitz

SAMUELFRENCH.COM   SAMUELFRENCH.CO.UK

ISBN 978-0-573-62669-2

www.SamuelFrench.com
www.SamuelFrench.co.uk

FOR PRODUCTION ENQUIRIES

UNITED STATES AND CANADA
Info@SamuelFrench.com
1-866-598-8449

UNITED KINGDOM AND EUROPE
Plays@SamuelFrench.co.uk
020-7255-4302

Each title is subject to availability from Samuel French, depending
upon country of performance. Please be aware that *LEBENSRAUM* may
not be licensed by Samuel French in your territory. Professional and
amateur producers should contact the nearest Samuel French office or
licensing partner to verify availability.

MUSIC USE NOTE

Licensees are solely responsible for obtaining formal written permission from copyright owners to use copyrighted music in the performance of this play and are strongly cautioned to do so. If no such permission is obtained by the licensee, then the licensee must use only original music that the licensee owns and controls. Licensees are solely responsible and liable for all music clearances and shall indemnify the copyright owners of the play(s) and their licensing agent, Samuel French, against any costs, expenses, losses and liabilities arising from the use of music by licensees. Please contact the appropriate music licensing authority in your territory for the rights to any incidental music.

IMPORTANT BILLING AND CREDIT REQUIREMENTS

If you have obtained performance rights to this title, please refer to your licensing agreement for important billing and credit requirements.

To countless unborn Jewish and German artists. Nie weider.

INTRODUCTION

A few years ago, my German play-agent reprimanded me, quite sternly, saying that I'd repeatedly rejected invitations to visit productions of my plays in Germany. He pointed out that my plays were getting quite popular in Germany, but that I was doing nothing to help him. Simply said, people knew my plays but didn't know *me*. I was actually quite surprised. I hadn't realized that I'd turned down any invitations to visit Germany at all ... well, maybe a few ... And then, I added it up. In recent years, by my own calculations, I'd found reasons not to visit Germany some fifteen times. In fact, I'd *never* seen a play of mine in German language. Never. Never isn't a lot.

I thought it through, starting from when I was a 5-year-old, in my bed at night in Wakefield, Massachusetts, thinking that the Nazis would be soon coming through my window to kill me and my family. But, that was 53 years ago. A few things have changed, since then.

So, okay, I accepted my agent's proposition for a whirlwind visit to some then-current German productions of my plays, and to some German theatres considering my plays, and to a couple of my German translators. My first stop would be Bonn, for an important production of "Park Your Car In Harvard Yard". And then, Cologne, where I would see an old friend (pen-pal variety) at WDR (Westdeutschen Rundfunk), a radio network that's done my plays over the past 25+ years. And then, Frankfurt, Hamburg, Berlin ...

In Bonn, first station of my particular cross, I had a drink with my play's producer, who told me that there would be a small press-conference, after that night's performance. Using a quickly-bought dictionary, I prepared a small speech, in German, saying how happy I was to be in Bonn, etc, etc. As I watched the performance, which struck me as being excellent, I wondered what the reaction would be to the lead-character's speech about being a Yankee-Jew. I didn't sit with held breath, I just *wondered*. In fact, the speech never got spoken. (At least, I didn't *think* it got spoken. I don't speak German. It's a language that's always seemed to me to be rather comical, so many *fahrt*-words ... I've always imagined Germans standing around on street-corners, laughing about how funny they sound.) Anyway, after the show, which got a strong and positive audience response, I stood with the actress, waiting for our press-conference to begin. Making friendly conversation (I thought) , I asked her, cautiously (I thought) ... "Did the old man ever make his speech about being a Yankee-Jew?"

... Her answer took my life around a corner I didn't even know was there ... "Oh, no!" she said. "You can't have Jews on stage in Germany. It doesn't smell good."

Smell good? *Smell* good? Before I could start to talk this out with her, the press conference began. I was introduced in glowing terms. I re-pocketed my little speech and in English (the language of International Business, which most everybody seems to speak in Germany), I said ... "Being in your country – hearing your language being spoken – is an act of heroism for me. It brings me back to when I was five years old, in Wakefield, Massachusetts, lying in my bed at night, thinking the Nazis were about to come through my window to kill me and my family ..." Needless to say, there have been more popular speeches made in Germany, before and after mine.

The next day, in Cologne, still extremely angry, I told the story to my WDR-friend, Angela, who was amazed, but smiled, knowingly, as if she had the answer that would calm me ... "The actress probably doesn't speak English very well. It was a problem of language, that's all ... The actress was trying to say was that a Jewish character on stage sends a German audience into thinking the play is about the Holocaust. And your play is not about the Holocaust. It would have confused them." This was not calming news.

In Berlin, a few days later, I stayed at the apartment of one of my German translators, Miriam Mueller. Miriam is the daughter of a highly-regarded German playwright, Harald Mueller (*"Totenfloss"*, *"Stille Nacht"*). Arnaud, her live-in boyfriend (now live-in husband), is French. Miriam speaks English. I speak English and French. We could all talk about this thing that happened to me ...

First off, Miriam told me that, growing up, she "didn't have any casual Jewish friends, whatsoever", meaning, no Jewish school-chums, no Jewish neighborhood kids. Why? "There were none. They were dead." In fact, Miriam told me that she didn't have any Jewish friends at all until she was in her twenties and went to translation school in London. And Arnaud talked about the guilt that young German people feel concerning what their parents and grandparents did more than 50 years ago ... and about the unthinkable pain young Germans have inherited ... The German legacy ...

We three stayed up most of the night, talking. I never slept. At 6 a.m., sleep-deprived, I left the apartment and took my morning run in the Charlottenberg *Shlosspark,* around the castle. I was obsessed by all this ... by Miriam's never having a Jewish friend ... by Jews being unknown, abstract, even to sophisticated people like the children of successful playwrights ... and by what Arnaud had said about the profound guilt Miriam and her young German friends feel, forced on them by parents and/or grandparents ... (Miriam told me she'd been given a name thought to be Jewish, because "My parents wanted to replace a dead Jewish child") ...

As I ran, I thought to myself, "If Jews are totally abstract and are causing young Germans so much guilt, it's only a matter of time before young Germans say to themselves "these abstract Jews are a major pain in the ass to me!" ... and here we go, again!" ...

And then, out of the sky and into my head came the first image of my play "Lebensraum" ... Germany's Chancellor wakes from a nightmare and calls a press conference that he promises will contain "the news of the Century". In front of politicians, citizens, reporters, radio microphones, television cameras, he speaks the following words to Germany: "We face the start of a new millennium ... a new beginning. As Chancellor of this great German republic, I extend an invitation to six million Jews from anywhere in the world to come to live their lives in Germany. I speak to you, now: You will be given citizenship and full privileges in this great nation. You will be German. It is my heartfelt desire to re-establish a Jewish community in Germany, and to reduce, as much as humanly possible, the immeasurable shame we Germans feel each day of our lives for what this country did to our German-Jewish neighbors, 60 years ago. What I am saying to you six million Jewish people is quite simple, really. Please, come home. Please."

As soon as I had the idea, I felt faint. I stopped running and grabbed hold of a bench, next to a small, rectangular trashcan upon which a Nazi *swastika* had been hand-drawn by magic-marker. I was weak, sweating. Suddenly, a pack of unattended dogs rushed past me, barking ferociously. At first, I thought I would die of fright. And then, I actually laughed aloud ... It was all so shabbily *theatrical.*

I ran back to Miriam's apartment and begun to write my ideas into my notebook. When Miriam and Arnaud woke, I told them my plan for the new play ... and that I might call it "Lebensraum" ... "Living Space" ... Hitler's initial promise to the German nation when he first set out to conquer the world. Miriam and Arnaud were instantly supportive.

I wrote the first draft of "Lebensraum", obsessively. I had been in the midst of writing a new play, "My Old Lady". I stopped work on that play ... and on the screenplay I was writing for the recent movie based on my play "North Shore Fish". In fact, I stopped almost everything in my life but for the writing of "Lebensraum". I read 15-20 new pages a week to the other playwrights of The New York Playwright Lab. I only half-listened to their criticism. In Sylvia Plath-speak, I was "seized by a savage God".

I gave the play an odd, theatrical form, calling for three actors to play some eighty characters. I felt that any play dramatizing Jews, Germans, the Holocaust, at this point in history, needed a fresh approach, both formally and substantially. Without realizing it at the time, I called for three actors who precisely fit the description of the main actors of the Hercub Company, with whom I have been working successfully during the past six years in France. It is they who are doing the European Premiere of "Lebensraum", at this moment, at Festival d'Avignon, in a translation they've created with my young friend Charlotte Vuarnesson. "Lebensraum" opened at Théâtre du Balcon, in Avignon, a week ago, to a packed house. I'm told there is a standing ovation, each night.

The World Premiere of "Lebensraum", was given, of course, at my own theatre, Gloucester Stage, in tandem with my other new play, "My Old Lady". Both plays brought tearful audiences to their feet ...; "My Old Lady" (*"Meine Alte Dame"*) will have its European premiere in Dortmund, Germany, in September; and the Gloucester Stage production of "Lebensraum", under Richard McElvain's inventive direction, will re-open in NYC at The Miranda Theatre in October. Several productions of "Lebensraum" are planned for Germany during the next few seasons.

For what it's worth, I am certain that at age 57, I somehow wrote my best work (thusfar) ... 30 years after "The Indian Wants The Bronx", "It's Called The Sugar Plum", "Line" and "Rats" opened, one after the other, in my incredible "First Season" as a produced playwright in New York City. But, in the end, it is quite difficult to comment intelligently on one's own work ... ie; what's important work, what's not important work. Such self-assessment feels wrong ... absurd ... like a snail explaining its shell ... except to say that it does often seem to me that all of life exists as preparation for the next day. All past is prologue. Such is the nature and condition of Hope. And, in the end, one cannot possibly have the fullest life without dreaming it, first. But, if we allow ourselves the dream, yes, oh, yes, all things are possible.

I.H., Gloucester, Mass., Summer, 1997

AUTHOR'S NOTE:

This play is designed to be performed by three actors on an essentially barren stage. Scenery should be limited to platforms, ramps, and racks draped with various costumes and props. I strongly suggest imaginative use of props and costumes to indicate character. Puppetry techniques, such as portraits with cut-out spaces for heads and hands, add-on fat stomachs, hand-held masks, and objects in miniature, should be liberally employed. Music should be used, throughout, to underscore action. Practical lighting – lamps turned on and off by the actors – can be freely used, in addition to conventional stage-lighting. In short, great invention is asked of you, in keeping this sometimes grim story forever entertaining.

THE PEOPLE OF THE PLAY:

ACTOR #1 *(Younger, Male)*
... Narrator; also plays Political Announcer, Steffen Von Menck, TV Talk Show Host, Götz Witzenbacher, Sammy Linsky, Zev Golem, Jacob Brontheim, High School Teacher, Pierre Chambray, Günter Friedlander, Sign-In Centre Clerk, Various Voices.

ACTOR #2 *(Older, Male)*
... Narrator; also plays Rudolph Stroiber, Gustav Giesling, Professor Viktor Spretz, Reverend Hans Schnabel, Michael Linsky, Rabbi Shlomo Brechtman, History Teacher, High School Teacher, Axel Rosensweig, Maximillian Zylberstein, Jacques Burstin, Ludwig Hess, Götz Burger, Sign-In Centre Clerk #2.

ACTOR #3 *(Younger, Female)*
... Narrator; also plays Eva Mueller, Bessie Mandelbaum, Gertrude Moskowitz, Millie Brontheim, Lizzie Linsky, Anna Giesling, High School Teacher, Berta Giesling, Reba Golem, Katrina Keitel, TV Interviewer, Rifka Borenstein, Fishpacker, Esla Krebs, Various Voices.

THE PLACE OF THE PLAY:

Various locations around the world, including Gloucester, Massachusetts, U.S.A., and Bremerhaven, Germany.

THE TIME OF THE PLAY:

The start of the 21st century.

(As audience enters theatre, the stage is illuminated by work-lights. The scenery is primarily wooden platforms and wooden racks, upon which hang various costumes, masks, props, etc. At curtain-time, STAGE MANAGER calls out from the booth ...)

STAGE MANAGER. *(Off)* Okay, actors ... The stage is yours. We're ready!

(Three actors enter and casually check their costumes and props. Eventually, they get into their starting-positions. ACTOR #2, lying on a ramp, center, is covered by a blanket by ACTOR #3, as if in bed. ACTOR #2 calls to STAGE MANAGER, off ...)

ACTOR #2. We're ready, stage manager!
STAGE MANAGER. *(Off)* Thank you. Stand by for music and lights. We're going.

(Lighting shifts, suddenly, from pre-show work-lights to dramatic stage-lighting. Music in, pulsating, nightmarish. ACTOR #2, grey-haired, 60-ish, is now sleeping, in the throes of a frightening dream. Suddenly, he screams out from his sleep. The play has begun.)
(Light up on ... ACTOR #1, an affable, handsome young man, who speaks to audience.)

ACTOR #1. At 3 a.m., Rudolph Stroiber woke from a most terrible nightmare. *(ACTOR #2 screams, again, sits up, sharply. Then, moves to platform, dresses in his next costume.)* Although it was Winter and his window was half open, his body was drenched with perspiration. He was trembling with excitement. He had formulated an astonishing plan.

11

(ACTOR #2 re-enters, as RUDOLPH STROIBER, carrying a framed "official" cut-out portrait through which his head and hands appear. He smiles a politician's smile ...)

ACTOR #2. Guten Morgen ... Guden Morgen ... Guden Morgen ...

ACTOR #1. Herr Stroiber called together his family, his closest friends, his most learned advisors, and the very highest leaders of the German government. Every newspaper, every radio and television network was in attendance for what Herr Stroiber announced would be "the news of the century". *(ACTOR #3 holds briefcase on shoulder as TV Camera, yells out countdown, "Finf, fier" She motions "3, 2, 1." ACTOR #1 continues ...)* Ladies and gentlemen, I give you Rudolph Stroiber, the Chancellor of the German Republic ...

(We hear ... applause, cheering.)

RUDOLPH STROIBER. We face the start of a new millennium ... a new beginning. As Chancellor of this great German republic, I extend an invitation to six million Jews from anywhere in the world to come to live their lives in Germany. I speak to you, now: You will be given citizenship and full privileges in this great nation. You will be German. It is my heartfelt desire to re-establish a Jewish community in Germany, and to reduce, as much as humanly possible, the immeasurable shame we Germans feel each day of our lives for what this country did to our German-Jewish neighbors, 60 years ago. What I am saying to you six million Jewish people is quite simple, really. Please, come home. Please.

(Lights crossfade to ... ACTOR #3, young blonde, blue-eyed, adorable; instantly appealing. She speaks directly to audience ...)

ACTOR #3. Herr Stroiber's speech ended as quickly as it had begun. At first, there was a shocked silence. And then, Steffen Von Menck, a senator from a suburb of Cologne, clapped his hands together, ten claps. He, alone, applauded. *(Light fades up on ... ACTOR #1, now playing VON MENCK. He claps his hands together, ten claps.)* After ten solitary claps, Herr Von Menck stopped. There was a most deafening silence ... *(Silence. ACTOR #1 drops a pin.)* ... Before the screams began.

(Silence. And then, on tape, we hear ... Shouts, crowds yelling.)

ACTOR #1. In Bremerhaven, Gustav Giesling, a dockworker and father of six, shouted into the microphone of a roving reporter from Westdeutscher Rundfunk ...

(Lights up, suddenly, on ... ACTOR #2 as GUSTAV GIESLING. ACTOR #3 shoves a microphone at him.)

ACTOR #2. *I'm* not shy. *I'll* tell you what's going on. I can't feed my children, that's whats going on! Last year, in my sector, alone, 900 dockworkers lost their jobs! In one year! I was one of the lucky ones! I kept my job, but, there's no work! There are no ships coming into port to load or unload! There are no fish, no containers, no work! I earned 10,000 marks, last year, before taxes, and my house-payments and car-payments, combined were *20,000* marks! Where do we put six million new people, Jews or not? I don't personally care if these six million are Jews or if they're monkeys ... Where do we put them, and how do they feed themselves?! ... Ask yourselves *that*?

ACTOR #1. In Dusseldorf, Frau Eva Mueller had a different sort of reaction, which she discussed on "Open Your Heart", a popular daytime television talk-show ...

(Light up on ... ACTOR #3 as EVA MUELLER, holds a framed TV-screen in front of her face, speaks ...)

ACTOR #3. I have three unmarried daughters. The oldest is 20, and the youngest is 17. Do you not think that Jews will be looking for young German girls to marry, as soon as they arrive? If you think they won't be, you are crazy! They will romance our young daughters, and do you know how sorry our daughters will feel for them, when they hear their sad stories? Their tears and their knickers will be on the ground in no time! ... I tell you, young German girls will be a prize for these Jews!

(ACTOR #1 sits facing EVA.)

ACTOR #1. Frau Mueller, it is a fact that, historically, Jews marry their own. Throughout history, since the bible, Jews marry Jews. I understand your anxiety, but, deep in your heart, won't you feel better about yourself if the shame we feel as a nation is lessened, if not erased?
ACTOR #3. What shame? *What shame?*

(Lights crossfade to ... ACTOR #2.)

ACTOR #2. At the University in Bonn, Viktor Spretz, Distinguished Professor of Psychology, stood before 200 of his university colleagues and delivered a hastily-written, deeply sincere paper on the events of the past two days. *(ACTOR #2 looks up at VIKTOR SPRETZ; taps microphone; speaks to people at rear of auditorium ...)* Can you hear me back there? Can you hear me? ...
STAGE MANAGER. *(Off)* Yuh, yuh, we hear you!
SPRETZ. Thank you. What I want to say to you wants to be said, calmly, without my worrying about projecting my voice like an actor. I want to speak to you, quietly, from my heart. Normally, I have no interest in politics. But, suddenly, what our government is proposing interests me, deeply. *(Takes notes from his pocket.)* I hope you won't think I'm in any way insincere because I have notes. I'll try not to read everything I say. I'll try to speak somewhat spontaneously, when it's ... How shall I say it? Appropriate. When it's appropriate. *(Clears his throat; reads ...)* This Republic has, for sixty years, been drowning in a sea of guilt. Especially our children ... our young people ... two generations against the Jewish people. In the last forty-eight hours, incredibly, a solution has come, not from our philosophers, not from our psychoanalysts, not from our artists, not from our writers, not from our clergymen, but from our *government!* We have been encouraged to welcome six million Jews to Germany ... to welcome them to live here among us as Germans ... as equals ... and to this, I say, emphatically, "yes"! ... How beautifully direct is this idea, how totally uncomplicated, how astonishingly achievable ...
ACTOR #3. Unnoticed, at first, in the center of the auditorium, Doctor Götz Witzenbacher, Vice-Chairman of the Psychology

Department, celebrated scholar of Freud and Wittgenstein, stood on his chair and took the chance of his life ...

(ACTOR #1 stands on a chair – if possible, in the center of the auditorium, amongst the actual theatre-audience – and gives the salute of the 3rd Reich ...)

ACTOR #1. Heil, Hitler! Heil, Hitler! Heil, Hitler!

ACTOR #3. What followed was a kind of mayhem. Doctor Witzenbacher was, at first, screamed at ... and then, he was applauded by a quartet of skinhead-students at the rear of the auditorium, but, then, he was pulled from the chair and punched by Helmut Vogel, a promising young professor from the University's History Department. Dr, Witzenbacher fell to the ground and he was stomped by several important young faculty-members, including professors of literature, science, and the plastic arts.

(ACTOR #2 throws ACTOR #1 to the ground and kicks him, viciously. Drumbeats, as WITZENBACHER dances being punched.)

ACTOR #2. *Pig! Pig!*

(On tape, we hear ... Shouts of anger and protest. WITZENBACHER is on the ground, now, on his back, center. ACTOR #3 approaches him, ripe tomato in her hand. ACTOR #2 covers SPRETZ with a white plastic sheet. And then ...)

ACTOR. #3. Dr. Witzenbacher's skull was crushed. He died, almost immediately.

(ACTOR #3 crushes the tomato. Its inner juice and pulp falls on to the white plastic sheet, which ACTOR #2 folds and removes.)

ACTOR #2. The crowd was astonished. No one knew what to do. They backed away from Dr. Witzenbacher's still-trembling body, leaving him alone in death, face down, in the center of the crowded auditorium.

ACTOR #3. Just three months earlier, Dr. Witzenbacher had been short-listed for the Nobel Prize in Science. He was a frequent guest on important German television panel-shows, and was well-known throughout the world as a liberal-minded German intellectual.

(ACTOR #1 rises; speaks to audience, directly, quietly ...)

ACTOR #1. What demon had seized Götz Witzenbacher? Was it a kind of momentary madness? Whatever it was, it had cost him his life. The academin community was shocked and outraged ... and profoundly sorrowful. At the funeral of Doctor Götz Witzenbacher, Reverend Hans Schnabel, a renowned Lutheran minister, added fuel to a fire that was already burning out of control ...

(ACTOR #2 steps forward, speaks as MINISTER at a funeral. Church music in ... under the scene.)

REVEREND SCHNABEL. Many of us have known Dr. Götz Witzenbacher for several years. We have known him as a great thinker, as a great writer, as a great pillar of our university community. I have personally known Herr Witzenbacher as a devoted father to his children, an exemplary husband to his wife, and as a man of God. His violent death leaves us stunned and confused. What our government has proposed will light the fuse of violence throughout the German Republic. I implore Herr Chancellor Stroiber and Herr Doctor Witzenbacher's death and to withdraw their invitation, immediately. When I speak against this issue, I am not speaking against Jews. I have no negative feelings about Jews. But, the manner in which our government is trying to undo sixty years in sixty minutes is unthinkable. Now, we must bury our friend Götz Witzenbacher. His four children are without a father. And this great German Republic is without one of its greatest thinkers. Let us bow our heads and pray.

ACTOR. #1. And now, the clergy-population of Germany was in a hideous flap. Most clergymen called for Herr Reverend Schnabel's immediate resignation from the altar. But, several ministers and church lay-people proclaimed Herr Reverend Schnabel "a modern-day German hero" ... a courageous speaker of what many came to know as "the great and undeniable German truth" ...

ACTOR #3. *(Carries a rubber fish, wiggles fish's mouth, "throws" her voice, as though fish is speaking ...)* In America, in Gloucester, Massachusetts, a fishing port, north of Boston, at land's end, Michael Linsky, an unemployed dockworker, spoke to his teenaged son.

ACTOR. #2. *(With working class Boston accent, as MIKE LINSKY ...)* I dunno, Sammy ... This offer could be wick'id appealing. I mean, we can't do worse than we're doin' here! You see what I'm sayin' on this?

ACTOR #1. *(As SAMMY, cap backwards; bouncing basketball ...)* Germany? Are you *crazy?* They speak *German* in Germany!

ACTOR #2. *(To audience, as NARRATOR.)* And in Tel Aviv, Israel, Bessie Mandelbaum, a survivor of Auchswitz, heard the news and wept ...

(ACTOR #3 wears dark shawl, as BESSIE MANDELBAUM ...)

BESSIE MANDELBAUM. My mother, my father, my two brothers, Edgar and Issac ... my little sister, Becca ... my cousins Asher, Yisak, Izzie, and Shem, my tante Rachael ...

ACTOR #2. *(To audience, as NARRATOR.)* South of Jerusalem, in Beersheva, Zev Golem, a high-ranking officer in the Israeli Army, heard the news over a meal of blini and smoked salmon and alerted his wife, and cautioned his wife, angrily ...

ACTOR #1. *(As ZEV GOLEM.)* Any Jews who go to live in Germany are fools. They are as good as dead. The Germans will finish the job, the first opportunity they have. These Jews will be shot in the back, the first time they try to take a stroll. No one will bury them. Their bodies will rot in the streets. Dogs and rats will eat the flesh from their bones! ...

ACTOR #3. *(To audience, as NARRATOR.)* And in Jerusalem, Rabbi Shlomo Brechtman read the news and called together a meeting of the most intelligent men and women of his congregation.

(ACTOR #2 enters as REB BRECHTMAN, wearing mask with Talmudic beard.)

BRECHTMAN. We must go. We must do this. We must bring our young people with us. We must reclaim this place for Jews.

ACTOR. #1. *(As NARRATOR.)* Not all of Reb Brechtman's friends agreed with him.

ACTOR. #3. *(As older woman, MRS. MOSKOWITZ.)* I would rather put a knife in my son's heart than send him to live among the Germans!

ACTOR #1. Gertrude Moskowitz, who lost her entire family to the ovens of Buchenwald, who was raped by Nazi soldiers at the age of twelve, was overcome by a savage rage she could not begin to control. Reb Brechtman tried to reason with her, but, to no avail ...

ACTOR #2. *(As REB BRECHTMAN.)* Mrs. Moskowitz, please! We must discuss this, together, intelligently.

ACTOR #3. *(Screams, as MRS. MOSKOWITZ.)* I'll gladly discuss this, intelligently, but, not with Nazi-lovers the likes of you, Herr Fuehrer Brechtman!

(MRS. MOSKOWITZ spits at BRECHTMAN, all three actors make a sound with sharp intake of breath. Then ...)

ACTOR #1. *(As NARRATOR.)* There was a terrible shocked silence after Gertie Moskowitz spat on Reb Brechtman. But, then Jacob Brontheim did something that made Mrs. Moskowitz's spittle seem like a gentle tear of regret. He walked to Reb Brechtman ... *(Walks to BRECHTMAN, grabs him by the throat ...)* ... Grabbed him by the throat ... *(Chokes BRECHTMAN.)* ... And begins to kill the kindly old Rabbi with his bare hands ... *(Yells, as BRONTHEIM.)* They tied my hands and legs and made me watch them rape my mother and my two sisters. There were ten of them. When they were done with their sex, they cut my mother's throat and they took my sisters away with them. I never saw my sisters, again. It took me three days to free my hands. For three days I watched my mother's dead body ...

(BRONTHEIM removes BRECHTMAN's beard and mask, which he now strangles, as though it were the old man, himself ...)

ACTOR #3. Suddenly, Brontheim's wife, Millie, began screaming and swatting at Brontheim, begging him to stop! *(Screams, as BRONTHEIM's wife ...)* Jacob, stop! Stop, Jacob, darling, stop!

ACTOR #1. But, Brontheim could not stop ... and Rabbi Brechtman's heart exploded. He slumped to the floor ...

(Beard and mask fall to the floor. The old Rabbi is dead.)

ACTOR #2. He's dead.
ACTOR #3. He's dead.

(ACTOR #2 steps forward, talks to audience, directly ...)

ACTOR #2. And so, within fifty hours of Rudolph Stroiber's invitation to the Jews, two intelligent men lay dead ... Götz Witzenbacher, who had dared to salute Hitler, and Rabbi Shlomo Brechtman, who had dared to think the return of six million Jews to Germany was a good idea.

(SPRETZ's hat and pipe are put in a bucket along with BRECHTMAN's mask and beard. Flash-paper, hidden in the bucket, is now ignited.)

ACTOR #3. In Gloucester, Massachusetts, Lizzie Linsky, née Elizabeth O'Donnell, wife of Michael Allen Linsky, made her husband say it to her, again ... *(As LIZZIE LINSKY.)* ... slowly, this time ...

ACTOR #2. *(With working class Boston accent, as MIKE LINSKY; speaks slowly ...)* I ... want us ... to move ... to Germany. *(Beat)* I'm serious, Lizzie! ... This offer makes sense on every level. You gotta' imagine they're gonna' come through with jobs, right? I mean, they can't pull six million new people into their country and not have work for us, right? So, why not? Nothin's happenin' here.

LIZZIE LINSKY. *(Same Boston accent.)* How can you even *think* about moving to Germany?! What's your mother gonna' say if you tell her we're moving halfway around the world?

MIKE LINSKY. German's not halfway around the world. It's maybe four thousand miles from here, that's all.

LIZZIE LINSKY. Fine. Four thousand miles. That's all.

MIKE LINSKY. I was thinking maybe my mother would, I dunno', maybe move with us kind of thing.

LIZZIE LINSKY. Did you, like, talk to your mother on this, already?

MIKE LINSKY. Course not! I wouldn't do that, Lizzie, would I? I know you and I've got to talk together on this, first.

LIZZIE LINSKY. I mean, what do we know about Germany? We'd be, like, *immigrants.* We'd be like the Italians and "Portegees" who come over here. You hear them in the Stop 'n' Shop tryin' ta' ask questions. Nobody can understand what they're sayin'! Nobody wants them here! ...

MIKE LINSKY. It's only a *language!* We'll study it. Bennie Krantz's brother went to music school in Germany. Bennie says everybody there speaks English, too.

LIZZIE LINSKY. Bennie said that?

MIKE LINSKY. Ask him. His brother didn't speak any German for the first year he was there and had no problems, whatsoever.

LIZZIE LINSKY. Why would Germans speak English?

MIKE LINSKY. It's the language of international business.

LIZZIE LINSKY. They speak *English*?

MIKE LINSKY. I'm thinking so positively on this, Elizabeth. I feel so *stupid* hanging around the house, no real job. It makes me feel stupid. Thinkin' about moving e*xcites* me. It could really be different.

LIZZIE LINSKY. What if it isn't?

MIKE LINSKY. Isn't different?

LIZZIE LINSKY. Isn't different. What if we move all the way there, and there's no work? Or supposing we just don't like it? What then?

MIKE LINSKY. We move back.

LIZZIE LINSKY. Just like that?

MIKE LINSKY. Just like that.

LIZZIE LINSKY. How? We swim?

MIKE LINSKY. We take a plane, same as we got there.

LIZZIE LINSKY. How are we even gonna' buy the plane-tickets in the first place?

MIKE LINSKY. We sell off the land my father left me.

LIZZIE LINSKY. You'd do that?

MIKE LINSKY. Sooner or later, I'm gonna' have to, anyhow. It's almost three years since I worked, full-time.

LIZZIE LINSKY. *(New tone; somewhat frightened.)* I can see what you're sayin'. I really can. It's just that it scares me. I'm not Jewish, so, I've got no particular gripe with Germans. It's just the pickin'-up-and-movin' part. Goin' someplace totally different. It really scares me, Mike.

MIKE LINSKY. It scares me, too, Lizzie. Don't think it doesn't, cause it does.

LIZZIE LINSKY. What about Sammy?

MIKE LINSKY. Sammy's a kid. He'll love it, ten minutes after he gets there. Kids learn languages a lot quicker than grownups. Everybody says that. Sammy'll be fine.

LIZZIE LINSKY. He's not gonna' want to go. He came running to me, first time you mentioned any of this to him!

MIKE LINSKY. He'll go. He's a kid. He's got no choice. If we go, he'll go.

(ACTOR #1 steps forward, as SAMMY. He is not happy. He yells ...)

SAMMY. *I won't! I won't! I fucking won't!*

MIKE LINSKY. You open up a filthy mouth like that in the house, I'll deck you! I swear ta' Christ!

SAMMY. It makes no sense!

MIKE LINSKY. It makes *plenty* of sense! There's work, there's money, and we're going. We're your mother and father and you're fifteen, so, you're going. For all I know, we won't like it and we'll be coming back in six months. Or maybe we'll like it. All's I know for sure is that we're gonna' try.

SAMMY. What if you like it and I don't? Then what?

MIKE LINSKY. You're gonna' have yourself a serious problem.

(Beat. And then ...)

ACTOR #3. In Bremenhaven, Gustav Giesling, was having a similar problem with his teenaged daughter, Anna.

ACTOR #2. *(As GIESLING; black moustache.)* I am your father.

I love you and I know what's best for you. I have *forbidden* you to go
to that meeting!

ACTOR #3. *(Speaks with sweet, gentle voice, as ANNA ...)* I don't
accept your ruling.

GUSTAV GIESLING. You don't *what*?

ANNA GIESLING. I don't accept your ruling. The meeting is
public and important. Almost everybody from my school will be there
– my teachers, my friends – and I'll be there, too. If you want to take
away my allowance, do it. If you want to scream until you give us both
headaches, do it. I'm going to the meeting.

(After a substantial pause, GUSTAV calls, upstage, to his wife ...)

GUSTAV GIESLING. *Berta!* Get in here and talk sense to your
daughter!

ACTOR #1. *(To audience, directly ...)* Anna Giesling was one of
four hundred and sixty Bremenhaven students who gathered in the
high school auditorium, that night, to hear their teachers explain
Chancellor Rudolph Stroiber's invitation to the Jews.

ACTOR #3. Like Anna, many students had no idea why
Chancellor Stroiber made such an offer to so *many* Jews. Anna had
nothing against Jews. In her entire life, she had never met a Jew. And,
as far as she knew, she had never read a story by a Jewish writer, or
even seen a play by a Jewish playwright, or heard a song by a Jewish
composer.

ACTOR #1. Thusfar, in her public-school education, when
Anna's teachers had reached the years 1933-through-1943, they'd told
their students ...

ACTOR #2. *(As a History Teacher.)* ... For an in-depth analysis of
this particular period of German history, you should talk to your
grandparents.

ACTOR #1. By contrast, many older high school students and
university students had heard and read so much about the Nazis and
the Holocaust, they were, frankly, bored by the very thought of it. But,
what they'd learned was distant and abstract, totally impersonal. The
real lessons were still as missing from their lives as were some six
million Jews missing from Eastern Europe.

ACTOR #3. Tonight, many of Bremenhaven's best and bravest teachers decided that these missing lessons should finally be taught, properly.

(The three actors now sit, side by side, center stage, as if students at a lecture. Their faces reflect the shock they feel.)

ACTOR #1. What the students heard that night, sent icy shivers through their hearts.

ACTOR #3. The students were young, and not from wealthy families. Most of them had never travelled outside of Germany.

ACTOR #2. They didn't know that most of the world hated them for what their grandparents had done.

ACTOR #1. They didn't know that they were being blamed for their nation's history.

ACTOR #2. Many of the students assembled had seen the American film "Schindler's List", a few years earlier, but, somehow, thought that the Nazis, as depicted in the film, represented only an isolated few Germans. Many had dismissed the film, altogether, as "Hollywood-Jewish propaganda". Again, the Holocaust was distant, abstract, impersonal.

ACTOR #3. Their teachers, brave men and women, all, told them everything they knew to be true. Not from books, but from their own lives. Stories of their parents and grandparents, stories of neighbors and family-friends, stories of normal German people.

(All three actors step forward as Teachers. They will speak in overlapping phrases, imaging their "memories" ...)

ACTOR #1. My father, Heinz Hinde, was assigned to a train depot that handled Jews being shipped to Buchenwald ...

ACTOR #2. My grandmother, Uta Krebs, called the police and told them that a family of Jews was hiding in her building ...

ACTOR #3. My mother and father assured me the Holocaust never happened. They assured me it was a Jewish invention ...

ACTOR #1. His job was closing the box-cars doors. He had a wooden bat to hit Jews who wouldn't move forward to make room.

ACTOR #2. The Jewish family had lived in my grandmother's building all their lives. She was jealous of them, because their children wore fancy clothes. She called the police.

ACTOR #3. The day I started kindergarten, my parents sat me down and told me that Jews were demons who printed money, and bought the Holocaust-Denial Law in Germany, so that no German could ever legally question "the Jewish lie".

ACTOR #1. He and his friends used to make jokes about the people they hit with their bats. They knew these people were being taken to the ovens. They knew.

ACTOR #2. She knew that this entire family would be murdered by the Nazis, but, she called the police, anyway.

ACTOR #3. They made me promise to tell my friends, but, never let on they were the ones who told me. Because of the Jewish law, I could get them in trouble.

ACTOR #1. When I was ten years old, I found a box of snapshots my father had taken during the War, and had saved as mementoes. There was picture after picture of Jewish people crammed into boxes, some with bleeding heads from being hit by my father and his friends.

ACTOR #2. My grandmother told me she had no regrets, whatsoever, and that she would gladly call the police and turn them in, again, now, if a similar occasion presented itself.

ACTOR #3. To this day, they still believe it is a Jewish lie. They believe it with all their hearts.

ACTOR #1. One by one, the teachers told their stories ... of their parents' and grandparents' unthinkable cruelty ...

ACTOR #2. ... Of how the German people were Hitler's partners in the slaughter of the Jews. Normal, upstanding German citizens were Hitler's most willing butchers.

ACTOR #3. Normal people ...

ACTOR #1. Normal people ...

ACTOR. #2. Normal people ...

ACTOR #3. My parents had a perfect marriage. They were loving, considerate, and sensitive. My childhood was ideal.

ACTOR #1. My father is a veterinarian. He loves animals. He's such a gentle, kindly man ... such a loving father.

ACTOR #2. My grandmother taught piano to children, all her life. Children loved her. Her school, Charlottenburg Kinder-Flügel, was quite well-known: There was always beautiful music playing in her house ... Bach, Beethoven, Brahms.

ACTOR #3. Every single one of us in this room has had someone in each of our families who we loved, deeply, who directly participated in the slaughter of six million Jews.

ACTOR #1. Normal people ...

ACTOR #2. Normal people ...

ACTOR #3. After the lecture, many students stayed in their seats and wept.

ACTOR #1. On the stage, their teachers embraced one another, each weeping with great relief that his or her darkest secret was so incredibly similar to the darkest secrets of all.

ACTOR #2. When Anna Giesling got home, later that night, she was a changed woman ...

ACTOR #3. *(As ANNA; sobbing.) How could you not tell me? How could you not tell me?*

ACTOR #2. I told you *not* to go to the meeting! I *told* you!

ACTOR #3. Mother? *(Sobs) Mother?*

ACTOR #1. Berta Giesling took her daughter in her arms, and held her, wordlessly. Together, they wept ... *(ACTOR #3 turns upstage, her back to the audience. She wraps her arms around her own body; "embraces" herself. ACTOR #2 watches, wordlessly.)* Gustav Giesling watched his wife and daughter weeping, together. He said nothing, but, he knew that his life was changing.

ACTOR #2. *(To audience, as NARRATOR.)* South of Jerusalem, in the center of Israel, in Beersheba, quite near the border of Jordan, Zev Golem's wife, Reba, cautiously gave her husband upsetting news from his family in America ...

ACTOR #3. *(As REBA GOLEM. She holds a letter in her hand.)* Your sister's son, the one who's living in Massachusetts ... married to the "schiksa" ... He's taking the offer.

ACTOR #1. *(As ZEV GOLEM.)* What offer? What are you telling me, Reba? What offer?

REBA. The, uh, German offer. That's what your sister says in her letter ... Her son, Michael ... he and his family.

ZEV. My sister's son is moving to Germany?

REBA. Soon. She says she knows six others ... children of her friends. Here, read ...

(REBA hands the letter to ZEV.)

    ZEV. No! ... I won't read it! ... No.

(ZEV bows his head. Kletzmer music in. Lights crossfade to ... ACTOR #2, downstage. He will now play two different characters, in rapid alternation, by literally changing hats. When he wears a tattered cloth cap, he will be playing an old Jew named MAXIMILLIAN ZYLBERSTEIN. When he wears a fancy dress-hat, he will be playing an old Jew named AXEL ROSENSWEIG.)
(Both men will speak English with essentially Eastern European accents, but with a trace of Australian accent, as well. As the scene begins, snow falls on to the two old men.)

    ZYLBERSTEIN. It's snowing, Rosensweig.

(ACTOR #2 changes from cap to hat. He is now playing ROSENSWEIG.)

    ROSENSWEIG. Yes, by goodness, it is, Zylberstein. I'm amazed.

(ACTOR #2 changes back from hat to cap; playing ZYLBERSTEIN, again.)

    ZYLBERSTEIN. Why you amazed, Rosensweig?

(Hat trick, again. And so it goes.)

    ROSENSWEIG. Because I didn't think it was snow that was falling on me. I thought it was something else.
    ZYLBERSTEIN. I know I'm going to be sorry for asking this, but, what did you think was falling on you, Rosensweig?
    ROSENSWEIG. Your bloody *dandruff*, Zylberstein! ...
    ZYLBERSTEIN. Here we go!
    ROSENSWEIG. I've told you fifteen times, this week, alone ... Head and Shoulders Shampoo! But, do you listen? Do you *ever* listen?
    ZYLBERSTEIN. *(Covers his ears.)* I'm not listening!

ROSENSWEIG. The "goyem" look at us, and what do they see? What do they *think*? ...

ZYLBERSTEIN. I'm not listening!

ROSENSWEIG. They're thinking "Fifty per cent of all Jews have dandruff"!

ZYLBERSTEIN. I'm hearing nothing!

(ROSENSWEIG sees that ZYLBERSTEIN has covered his ears. He is disgusted. He harumphs, gruffly.)

ROSENSWEIG. *Harumph!*

(The old Jews freeze, as ACTOR #3 steps forward, addresses audience as NARRATOR.)

ACTOR #3. In Australia, a tiny Northern village in the Tabeland, there lived two old Jews ... Zylberstein ... *(ACTOR #2 dons ZYLBERSTEIN's cap.)* And Rosensweig ... *(Cap changes to dress-hat.)* Rosensweig and Zylberstein were both concentration-camp survivors. When the war ended, the concentration camps were opened and survivors were released. Both men had lost everything ... Family, homes, all worldly possessions.

ACTOR #1. With funds from the American Joint Distribution Committee, both men were went to Australia to live.

ACTOR #3. By chance, they were settled in the same tiny village of fifty families, one hundred miles north of Cairns.

ZYLBERSTEIN. Rosensweig opened the village's only general store and fleeced everybody, charging way too much for everything he sold. But, people had no choice, and the "mumzer" made a fortune!

(Cap change to dress-hat.)

ROSENSWEIG. Zylberstein, the "putz", could never learn to speak a good English. He opened a business as a Mr. Fix-It. He should have called his business "Mr. Break-It-Worse"! He could never keep a dime in his pocket for more than five minutes, so, he ended up bumming money from Rosensweig.

ACTOR #1. They were the only Jews in the entire area, so, they were forced into a workable "enemyship", which has lasted, so far, for nearly sixty years.

ACTOR #3. They hated each other! ...

ACTOR #1. In their way.

ACTOR #3. Their personalities were as different as different can be.

ACTOR #1. Rosensweig was compulsively neat, never seen without a fresh white shirt and a tightly-tied necktie.

ACTOR. #3. Zylberstein was, in one-word euphemism ...

ZYLBERSTEIN. ... *Relaxed.*

ACTOR #3. His clothing was constantly spotted with meals from a fortnight earlier.

(ZYLBERSTEIN finds, speck of dried food on his trousers; eats it.)

ACTOR #1. He often forgot to wear his socks.

ROSENSWEIG. Where are your socks?

ZYLBERSTEIN. On my feet.

ROSENSWEIG. They certainly are not!

ZYLBERSTEIN. They certainly are!

ROSENSWEIG. They certainly are not!

ZYLBERSTEIN. *(Looks down. No socks.)* They were there, this morning.

ACTOR #1. Each of them bore his history, quite differently. Rosensweig suffered, quietly. If the subject of the War (of, God forbid, the Camps) ever arose, Rosensweig had a ready response.

ROSENSWEIG. We don't talk of those times. Those times are passed.

ACTOR #3. But, Zylberstein constantly tried to joke the horror out of his aching memory.

ACTOR. #1. Zylberstein was a neverending symphony of Holocaust jokes.

ACTOR #3. Witness Zylberstein's favorite joke.

(ACTOR #2 steps forward, as ZYLBERSTEIN ... tells a joke.)

ZYLBERSTEIN. Two Jews, Goldberg and Finkle, survived Buchenwald, together. Goldberg settled in New York City, and made millions. Finkle settled in Russia, and had a miserable life. A few years ago, Goldberg had to go on a business trip to Moscow. Because of the time-change, he woke at 5 a.m., and couldn't get back to sleep. Having nothing better to do, he takes a walk through the empty streets of Moscow. He spots an old man walking in the opposite direction, and he's positive it's Finkle. Suddenly, a KGB van pulls up to the curb and six KGB men get out, grab Finkle, and *boomie-boomie-boomie!* They beat Finkle to a bloody pulp. Then, the KGB men drive away in their van as quickly as they had come, leaving Finkle for dead, face down on the pavement. Goldberg runs across the street and kneels beside Finkle. He cradles the old Jew in his arms, and whispers to him, gently ... "Finkle, Finkle, open your eyes! It's me, Goldberg, from Buchenwald!" Finkle opens his eyes, looks up. And he murmurs to Goldberg, smiling, happily ... *(Joyously; compared to life in Moscow, a cherished memory.)* ... "Ahhhhhhh, Bushenwald! Those were the days!" ...

(ACTOR #2 changes cap for hat; speaks, now, as ROSENSWEIG.)

ROSENSWEIG. That is not a joke, Zylberstein. That is an *abomination!*
ZYLBERSTEIN. *(Flatly Beckettian.)* If you don't laugh, you cry.
ROSENSWEIG. I laugh when things are funny.
ZYLBERSTEIN. What's funny?
ROSENSWEIG. *Things* are funny.
ZYLBERSTEIN. What things?
ROSENSWEIG. When you see me laughing, you'll see what things.
ZYLBERSTEIN. I've known you for fifty-six years, Rosensweig. I've never once seen you laugh.
ROSENSWEIG. Very few things have been funny.
ACTOR #3. And then, without warning, Zylberstein said the first thing he had ever said to make Rosensweig laugh ...
ZYLBERSTEIN. I'm taking the Germans up on their offer, Rosensweig. I'm moving to Germany.

ROSENSWEIG. Excuse me?

ZYLBERSTEIN. You can't hear? You've got waxy ears? I', taking the Germans up on their offer. I'm moving to Germany.

ACTOR #1. And for the first time since 1937, since the Nazis entered his house and killed his father *(Drumbeat)*, mother *(Drumbeat)*, sisters *(Drumbeat)*, brothers *(Drumbeat)*, Grandmother and Grandfather *(Drumbeat)*, Axel Rosensweig rolled back his head, and laughed.

(ROSENSWEIG has a painted reaction to each item in NARRATOR's list, above. But, then, he laughs, lightly, at first. His laughter grows, joined by grotesque, "fun-house" laughter from other actors. It stops, suddenly. And then ...)

ACTOR #3. The first Jews to arrive in Germany under the new "Jewish Homecoming Law" were two Frenchmen from Nancy, in the north of France. They arrived in Bonn, a day before the government's official welcoming ceremony, and reported to Project homecoming's sign-in station, set up in a lovely house that had been Beethoven's birthplace.

(ACTOR #1 steps forward, as PIERRE CHAMBRAY, a flamboyantly gay young Frenchman; wears bright beret.)

PIERRE CHAMBRAY. Je m'appelle Pierre Chambray. Ahhh, mais, oui! ... Je m'excuse. Il faut que je parle votre langue. *(Hesitantly...)* I am ... named ... Pierre Chambray.

(ACTOR #2 steps forward as JACQUES BURSTIN, Pierre's gay lover. He wears a matching beret.)

JACQUES BURSTIN. And I am Jacques Berstin. Pierre and I are married.

(PIERRE and JACQUES kiss, coquettishly.)

PIERRE CHAMBRAY. Jacques and I have been married depuis longtemps.

JACQUES BURSTIN. Almost ten years.

PIERRE CHAMBRAY. We are here to live.

ACTOR #3. *(Silent scream. Then ...)* There was an astonished silence, broken by Katrina Keitel, 1st Assistant to Dr. Ludwig Hess, Rudolph Stroiber's most-trusted friend and Executive Chairman of "Project Homecoming". Katrina stepped forward and saved the moment, graciously ...

(Changes voice; now speaks as KATRINA KEITEL, puts on band embossed with word "WILLKOMMEN".)

KATRINA. We are thrilled that you have chosen Germany as your new home.

PIERRE CHAMBRAY. *(Completely unable to understand what KATRINA has said.)* De quoi vous parlez? *(To JACQUES.)* Qu'est-ce qu'elle raconte?

JACQUES BURSTIN.*(Smiling broadly.)* I am ... Jacques Burstin ... and he is Pierre Chambray.

PIERRE CHAMBRAY. We are married.

JACQUES BURSTIN. We come to live here.

PIERRE CHAMBRAY. Nous sommes Juives ...

JACQUES BURSTIN. Ahh, ouais! C'est ça! We are ... Jewish!

(JACQUES and PIERRE kiss each other, again, happily.)

ACTOR #3. While Kartina Keitel continued to speak, Project Homecoming's Executive Chairman, Dr. Ludwig Hess, an enormously fat man, who had, thusfar, remained silent, with his eyes and mouth opened to their wisest, extricated himself from the ceremony, hastily improvising a universally acceptable reason to leave ...

(ACTOR #1 enters as DR. LUDWIG HESS. He carries/wears his "official" portrait, padded with enormously fat stomach. HESS's head and hands poke through cut-out holes. He speaks ...)

ACTOR #1. I have to pee.

(HESS runs two full circles around the stage, in a mad sprint. He holds his belly with both hands.)

ACTOR #3. Despite his remarkable corpulence, Dr. Hess sprinted, non-stop, from Project Homecoming's headquarters, across the market-square, to Project Homecoming's main office in the baroque 15th-century building once occupied by radical German students protesting the War in Viet Nam. Chancellor Stroiber was there, confronted by a stack of two hundred and sixty thousand Citizenship Applications.
DR. HESS. Rudolph! Rudolph! The first two Jews are gay!

(ACTOR #1 looks up. He, too, wears his "official" portrait. He speaks as STROIBER ... tired, annoyed.)

RUDOLPH STROIBER. I'm sure they are. Why wouldn't they be?
DR. HESS. No, no, no! They're French queers, Rudolph! They're holding hands and kissing!

(STROIBER realizes what is being said. He and HESS share a scream.)

ACTOR #3. Within the hour, Jacques' and Pierre's immigration-papers were less in order than they had seemed to be at the outset. They were sent home to Nancy ... driven, in fact, in Chancellor Stroiber's own white limousine.

(ACTOR #3 takes a toy limousine, looks into windows. PIERRE and JACQUES sitting in chairs, acting as if they are on the rear seat of the limo. They giggle; hold hands, thrilled to be in a limo.)

PIERRE CHAMBRAY. C'est vachement chic.
JACQUES BURSTIN. Oui. Trés agréable.
KATRINA KEITEL. *(Into windows of toy limo.)* Uhhh ... C'est juste une toute petite formalité de plus avec vos documents d'immigration. *(Then, to audience, in own voice ... ACTOR #3:)*

Translation: There's just one more little formality with your immigration documents. *(As KATRINA ...)* Ce n'est pas du tout grave! On vous revoit, ici, dans deux semaines. *(In her own voice, to audience.)* Translation: It's not at all serious. We'll see you back here, again, in two weeks.

PIERRE CHAMBRAY. Oui, d'accord! A dans deux semaines! Merci!

JACQUES BURSTIN. Merci. A dans deux semaines!

KATRINA KEITEL. Au revoir, Jacques! Aur revoir, Pierre!

JACQUES & PIERRE. *(In unison.)* Au revoir, Katrina!

JACQUES BURSTIN. Elle est mignonne!

PIERRE CHAMBRAY. Elle est adorable! Elle est chou!

(Sounds of limo racing away, tires screaching, hurling down road ...)

ACTOR #3. *(To audience, as NARRATOR.)* Dr. Hess personally hand-chose the "official" first arrivals. He settled on an American-Jewish family and introduced them to the country on national television.

(LINSKY FAMILY holds TV "frame" in front of their faces. They are being telecast, nationally. ACTOR #2 leans forward into TV frame, speaks with working class Boston accent, as MIKE LINSKY...)

MIKE LINSKY. Hi. Michael Linsky. I'm really, really, uh, honored.

(ACTOR #1 leans forward, speaks with similar accent, as SAMMY ...)

SAM LINSKY. Sam Linsky ... I just wanna' go on record as saying I'm here because my parents made me come here! I ...

(ACTOR #3, as LIZZIE LINSKY, saves the moment, shoves SAMMY out of frame ...)

LIZZY LINSKY. *I'll talk, Sammy!* ... Hi, I'm Liz Linsky!

Michael's wife and Sammy's mom. I just want to say that we are truly
thrilled to be the first Jewish family to be welcomed to Germany in
your Project Homecoming. We are all pretty scared. It's new and we
don't speak German. *Obviously.*

MIKE LINSKY. But, we're gonna' learn! ...

LIZZIE LINSKY. We're gonna' *try* to learn.

*(SAMMY is bored, picks his nose, off-camera. We hear ... STAGE
MANAGER as TV INTERVIEWER, off.)*

TV INTERVIEWER'S VOICE. What kind of music do you like
Sammy?

SAM LINSKY. Beastie Boys ... Luscious Jackson ... Smashing
Pumpkins are totally cool ...

TV INTERVIEWER'S VOICE. And you, Frau Linsky. What are
your favorite pastimes?

LIZZIE LINSKY. Me? Oh, well, I'm into aerobics and horseback
riding. I love to ride. My family comes first, of course. We do a lot of
things, together ... as a family. Course, this is the biggest thing we've
ever done, together ... as a family ... Movin' here. I hope we make
some friends.

TV INTERVIEWER. Herr Linsky, could you tell us about
yourself?

MIKE LINSKY. Oh, yuh, sure ... First off, I guess, I am a lumper.
That's what you call "docker". I grew up in a fishing town in
Massachusetts. My father was a fisherman. I started working on the
docks when I was maybe eight or nine ... with my father. I started
lumpin' when I was about fourteen. I was always a strong kid. I liked
the physical, outdoor life kinda' thing. I also liked earning "the big
bucks" ... The money. *(Smiles at LIZZIE.)* Lizzie and I went all
through school, together, 1st grade right through high school. Our
fathers fished together for years and years. Lizzie – Elizabeth – she's
not Jewish. We're bringing Sammy up Jewish, though. He was Bar
Mitzvahed, back home, at the local synagogue, same as me. And
Lizzie comes to synagogue with us on the High Holiday. She fits in
easy. *(Beat)* We're very proud to be the first family welcomed to
Germany under this Project Homecoming. I'm praying that there's

work for me in my field ... on the docks. I love my work. It all dried up back home. Truthfully, I was out of work for the last couple of years. I'm praying things are better here. That's why we came. *(Smiles)* I'm a hard-worker, I'm honest ... and now, I'm here.

ACTOR #3. *(Speaks to audience, as NARRATOR.)* The Linsky family's first national TV appearance was an estimable success. Mike seemed no different from any German dock-worker; Elizabeth came across as bright and kind and sexually non-threatening. Sammy was an instant heart-throb for high school girls all over Germany.

ACTOR #1. Germans like Americans, and they liked the Linsky family, enormously.

ACTOR #3. Chancellor Rudolph Stroiber's popularity rating went up six points in one day.

ACTOR #2. *(As STROIBER, wearing portrait, giving interview.)* It is too soon for self-congratulations. All we know is that the first family is here, and they are nice people.

ACTOR #1. *(As NEWSMAN at press conference.)* Herr Chancellor Stroiber, how long do you think it will take before six million new Jewish citizens are fully integrated into German life?

RUDOLPH STROIBER. Truthfully? Years and years. We can bring the people here, we can help get started with their lives, but, full integration – the *reunion* that is my dream – that is a matter of spirit. That is a matter of time.

ACTOR #3. The Linskys were located in Bremenhaven. Mike was given one of the few full-time jobs on the Bremenhaven docks.

(ACTOR #3 changes voice to TV INTERVIEWER.)

TV INTERVIEWER. Herr Linsky, how is it going?

MIKE LINSKY. It's going really well! I was scared stiff about the language part of it, but, ya' know, it turns out that lumpin' is lumpin'. I mean, the containers come in and they've got to be unloaded. It's pretty much exactly the same here as it was back home. So, I do my work. If something complicated comes up, I watch the other guys, and I just copy what they're doin' ...

(ACTOR #1 enters with pen and paper, gets LINSKY's autograph.)

ACTOR #1. Danke.

MIKE LINSKY. Bitte. *(To camera.)* Hey, I'm workin'! I'm happy

ACTOR #3. *(As NARRATOR.)* Most of Germany applauded Mike
Linsky. They liked him. They liked his New England work-ethic, his
American openness. And they especially liked what they came to call
his "Judish Bärme" ... his "Jewish warmth".

ACTOR #1. The image of the Linsky family's successful relocation
was telecast around the globe. Within two weeks of their arrival in
Germany, a million five hundred thousand other Jewish families
inspired by the Linskys, made application for German citizenship.

ACTOR. #2. One million eight hundred and seven thousand people
had arrived in Germany, already, to live their new lives.

ACTOR #1. *(As PIERRE ...)* Including Pierre ...

ACTOR #2. ... And Jacques!

(ACTORS #1 and #2, enter. They wear berets, hold hands ...)

PIERRE CHAMBRAY. *(Smiling brightly.)* Coucou! C'est nous!

JACQUES BURSTIN. *(Smiling brightly.)* Coucou! Nous somme
là!

ACTOR #3. But, everyone in Germany was not smiling.

ACTOR #1. *(As FRENZIED GOVERNMENT WORKER, wearing
official portrait ...)* Chancellor Stroiber, I'm so sorry to interrupt your
conference, but, we're having a problem with the *Jews.*

RUDOLPH STROIBER. What is it?

FRENZIED GOVERNMENT WORKER. There are approximately
five hundred thousand new Jewish citizens with no place to sleep
tonight.

RUDOLPH STROIBER. Get them hotel rooms.

FRENZIED GOVERNMENT WORKER. Who will pay for that?

RUDOLPH STROIBER. Ask the hotels to donate their empty
rooms. If they refuse, get the best price you can and the government will
pay.

FRENZIED GOVERNMENT WORKER. Yes, sir. I'll do my best
sir.

ACTOR. #3. In Bremenhaven, an outraged Gustav Giesling made
his presence felt at a meeting of unemployed dock-workers.

(ACTOR #2 steps forward as GUSTAV GIESLING; raises his hand ...)

GUSTAV GIESLING. I'd like to speak. For those of you here I don't know, my name is Gustav Giesling. I was born in Bremenhaven, three streets away from here, and I've worked on the docks all my life ... well, since high school ... I was Vice-Chairman of the Dockers' Union for ten years. I've been a paid-up Union member for nearly thirty-five years. What I'm going to say, now, will not be popular.

ACTOR. #3. The membership leaned forward in their seats. Over the years, they'd known Giesling to be a hard worker, and a brutally-honest man, afraid of absolutely nothing.

GUSTAV GIESLING. What my father did in the War was his affair, not mine. I was born in 1949, into the worst possible chaos. When I was 16, to find a job was next to impossible. I found a job. Here. On the docks. I worked to make this country as great as it is, today. I intend to work to *keep* this country great. If our government wants to give our country away to six million Jews without jobs, I say "No!" ... I say "Stop!". I say "There are six million *Germans* without jobs. Take care of Germans, first!"

(On tape, we hear ... cheers and applause from two hundred people.)

ACTOR #3. Gustav Giesling's meeting was but one of a thousand similar meetings taking place in Germany, that night. Unemployed German workers were outraged that their government would create jobs for Jews, instead of creating them for Germans. Worse, in some instances, German workers were being *replaced* by Jews.

(ACTOR #1 steps forward, as GÜNTER FRIEDLANDER, wearing a cashmere overcoat draped over his shoulders. He smokes "two" Havana cigars, at the same time; approaches MIKE LINSKY, smiling ...)

GÜNTER FRIEDLANDER. Guten Morgen. You're Mike Linsky?

MIKE LINSKY. Yuh. I am.

GÜNTER FRIEDLANDER. Sehr erfreut. I'm Günter Friedlander. I own the docks.

MIKE LINSKY. Oh, *hiiiii!* I've heard your name.

(They shake hands.)

GÜNTER FRIEDLANDER. I want you to know that I'm really happy you're working here.

MIKE LINSKY. I'm really happy, too. Thanks.

GÜNTER FRIEDLANDER. You're kind of a star.

MIKE LINSKY. Oh, God, well, not really. I mean, I didn't do anything to, you know ...

GÜNTER FRIEDLANDER. Business is actually *up.* We're getting two more container-ships, this week, than we got, last week.

MIKE LINSKY. That's *great!*

GÜNTER FRIEDLANDER. I think it's mostly your doing.

MIKE LINSKY. How could that be?

GÜNTER FRIEDLANDER. I think it would be good for everybody if I pushed you up front a little.

MIKE LINSKY. How so?

GÜNTER FRIEDLANDER. I just had a TV-reporter in my office asking how you were doing. I told him we're thinking of promoting you.

MIKE LINSKY. Are you kidding?

GÜNTER FRIEDLANDER. I'd like to bring you into the office, maybe team you with sales-people. I know you can't really speak a lot of German, yet, so, we'll have to ...

MIKE LINSKY. Please, don't! ... I don't want to be inside. I want to stay outside.

GÜNTER FRIEDLANDER. You do?

MIKE LINSKY. I do. I appreciate what you're saying and all, but, I want to stay working outside.

DOCKOWNER. How about crew chief?

MIKE LINSKY. How so?

GÜNTER FRIEDLANDER. When I tell the TV-reporter you've turned me down for the office job, I want to be able to tell him something else is happening ... some other kind of promotion.

MIKE LINSKY. God! Crew chief would be *great!* What about the boys?

GÜNTER FRIEDLANDER. Are you kidding? The boys love you!

ACTOR #3. Herr Friedlander was right. Most of Mike Linsky's co-workers adored Mike. He worked hard, and he was, after all, a celebrity. But, Götz Burger, who was being replaced by Mike as Crew Chief, was less than adoring.

ACTOR #2. *(As eye-patched GÖTZ BURGER ...) This is a gewalttätigeit! An outrage!*

GÜNTER FRIEDLANDER. Götz, for God's sake, calm yourself! You'll burst a blood-vessel! I'm not taking any money away from you! I'm just putting you back in the crew for a while.

(ACTOR #3 enters, as sexy SECRETARY, with coffeepot.)

SECRETARY. More coffee, Herr Friedlander?
GÜNTER FRIEDLANDER. Bitte.
SECRETARY. Guten tag, Herr Burger.
GÖTZ BURGER. Guten tag, Frau Jauslin.

(SECRETARY refills mugs; exits.)

GÜNTER FRIEDLANDER. This will all blow over. For the moment, the Jews are very, very popular. We happen to have a very famous one, and business happens to be picking up. For the good of the dock – for you fellow workers – let this happen! It's my right as dock-owner to make it happen, with your blessing or without your blessing. Give this thing your blessing, Götz. Use your brain. Be smart.

GÖTZ BURGER. *No! ... I will not!*

ACTOR #3. But, the dock-owner did indeed have the right to replace a crew chief. And replace he did. While Michael Linsky was telling his wife Elizabeth his good news, and while Götz Burger was telling his wife Dunja his bad news, Sammy and Anna were meeting for the very first time ... *(Smiling at audience.)* ... As you must have known, all along, would happen.

SAM LINSKY. Hi. Do you, uh, speak any English?
ANNA GIESLING. I do, yes.
SAM LINSKY. Great! That's a major relief!

ANNA GIESLING. Why?

SAM. 'Cause, I've been staring at you in Biology class, non-stop, for about three days, and I was really hoping you'd, you know, speak English.

ANNA. Well, I do.

(An embarrassed pause.)

SAM. That's great. I'm Sam Linsky.

ANNA. I know. Everybody know that. I mean, all you have to do is turn on your TV, or read the local newspaper.

SAM. I guess.

ANNA. I'm Anna Giesling.

SAM. I know. I copied your name down from your Biology paper.

ANNA. I saw you doing that, yuh. *(Beat)* Do you speak any German, yet?

SAM. Not too much. Just the basics. Like, Where's the bus to Frederickstraße ... *Wo fährt (Excuse me.) ein Bus ab Frederickstraße?* I had to learn that, first day, or I never would have gotten home from school. I also know *"Wann fährt (Excuse me) der nächste Bus?"* ... When's the next bus? And basic food-German. *"Ich hätte gern Schinkenspeck, Hackfleisch"* ...

ANNA. You eat *Schinkenspeck?*

SAM. Yah, yah ... *Schinkenspeck.* Every morning, with my eggs. *Schinkenspeck's* a totally funny word. German's full of funny words. Sometimes. I think Germans must stand around laughing about how funny they sound.

ANNA. *(Pronouncing "Fährt" correctly.)* Is that why you say "excuse me" after you say "fährt"?

SAM. "Fährt"? Is that how you say it? "Fährt"? Oh, *God!*

ANNA. I thought Jews were against eating *Schinkenspeck?*

SAM. I dunno. I guess. We eat it. Maybe 'cause my mother's not Jewish. She does the cooking. 'Course, my father's Jewish, and he always eats it, too. But, he's not religious at all. I am. Religious. Not too much, but, more than my father. 'Course. I throw back the old *Schinkenspeck,* same as him. We call it "bacon".

ANNA. I know. Bacon.

SAM. I've been eating bacon and eggs with my father, at four o'clock, every morning, ever since I can remember.

ANNA. You get up at four in the morning?

SAM. For breakfast with my dad. Then, he goes to work and I go back to bed, till I have to get up for school. My mother does the same deal ... up at four, goes back to sleep, till she has to get up at seven-thirty with me. It's totally ridiculous.

ANNA. We all get up at Four, same as your family. My father has to be to work at five, too.

SAM. What's he do?

ANNA. He's a docker. He works on the docks, unloading ships. Same dock as *your* father.

SAM. You're kidding?

ACTOR #2. *(To audience, as NARRATOR.)* Sam and Anna stayed together, for the next four hours, discovering all their amazing similarities – and differences. They skipped taking *der nächste Bus ab Frederickstraße,* opting to walk, together, talking ... falling in love.

ANNA. Do you really like the Beastie Boys?

SAM. *(Pimp-walks.)* They're genius! They totally rule!

ANNA. Maybe I'll give them another try.

SAM. I'll take you through a couple of cuts on "Paul's Boutique". You've got to have the lyrics out, when you listen the first five or six times, otherwise, you can't understand anything they're saying.

ANNA. That's exactly what happened to me! I couldn't hear the words so well.

SAM. I'll take you through it.

ANNA. That's be great. I could help you with extra German lessons, if you'd like.

SAM. You could? You would? *Really?*

ANNA. Sure.

ACTOR #2. *(To audience, as NARRATOR.)* Sam stared at Anna. He wanted to kiss her more than he wanted to breathe. He didn't dare. He breathed, instead.

SAM. *(Exhaling)* You're really beautiful.

ANNA. I'm *not!*

SAM. Oh, God, you so totally *are!* Back home, you'd be elected head cheerleader, hands down. *Shit!* I mean, *Sheisse!* That's so dumb, what I just said!

ANNA. I don't know what what you said means.

SAM. Trust me.

ANNA. I do trust you.

ACTOR #2. What Anna said next took Sam by surprise.

ANNA. You're very handsome, Sam.

SAM. Go on!

ANNA. I can't go on. That's it. That's all I have to say. I guess you hear you're handsome a lot ... from a lot of girls.

SAM. Just you and Elizabeth.

ANNA. Who's Elizabeth.

SAM. My mother. Oh, yuh, Selma, too ... My Grandmother. She always pinches my cheek ... *(Pinches his own cheek, imitates his Grandmother's voice ...)* Oy, Sammy, you're handsome! *(Smiles)* Those three girls ... Liz, Selma, and, now, you.

ACTOR #2. It is often said that great loves are mad ein their differences, not in their similarities. Sam never knew what Anna was going to say next. She often shocked him.

ANNA. Do you think we should stop talking and do the kissing? I don't know your morality-position on boy and girls kissing during their first meeting.

SAM. I'm American! I have no morality-position! ... It's not a subject that comes up a lot. Oh, yuh ... There was this one girl, Maxine, who moved into town in 8th grade. I kissed Maxine the first time *we* met. We were walking home across the beach and I, uh, kissed her.

ANNA. What happened?

SAM. She stopped talking to me. She started walking home with Brian O'Donnell.

ACTOR #2. Sam asked Anna if she'd had a lot of boyfriends.

ANNA. Not at all. I'm not allowed to have boyfriends.

SAM. Really? Are you, like, some kind of German *nun?*

ANNA. *(Laughs)* No, my father's really strict with us.

ACTOR #2. Anna told Sam about her parents, about her brothers and sisters. And then, Sam talked about *his* family ...

SAM. I'm an only child. I had a brother, but he died.

ANNA. Oh, no!

SAM. It was before I was born. He drowned when he was little. He fell off my uncle's boat. He was two, I think ...

ANNA. How terrible!

SAM. Deep down, I always thought it was a good thing for me. My parents really wanted me. They kept telling me that.

ACTOR #2. Anna asked Sam if being an only child put a lot of pressure on him ...

SAM. Not really. Maybe. I guess it made me learn how to be a good swimmer.

(ANNA laughs.)

ANNA. That's *terrible,* to say that! ... You're so funny.

SAM. You think so?

ANNA. I *know* so.

SAM. Then it's definitely okay for us to kiss.

ANNA. Because I laugh at your jokes?

SAM. Because you laugh at my jokes.

(They kiss.)

ACTOR #2. And that's how Sam Linsky, American, Jewish, and Anna Giesling, German, Lutheran, came to kiss a perfect first kiss ... full of exploration, full of gentleness and caring ... and totally without guilt.

(They break from their kiss.)

SAM. Oh, God! That was really good! I'm really glad we did that!

ANNA. Me, too! Before the first kiss, you're always worrying about whether to do the kissing or not.

SAM. It was definitely the main thing on *my* mind, I can tell you that!

ANNA. I always think, "After you kiss the boy, you can begin to talk and get to know each other!" ... You must promise you'll never tell my father I said any of this!

SAM. I promise. As long as you promise to never tell my grandmother you're German.

ANNA. What should I tell her I am?

SAM. We'll think of something. Maybe Korean. How do you feel about *second* kisses?

ANNA. Very favorably.

(They kiss, again. As soon as their lips meet ... Lights shift to ... ACTOR #2, downstage ...)

ACTOR #2. At the very moment Anna and Sammy's lips made contact for the 2nd time, Max Zylberstein arrived at Project Homecoming's sign-in center in Bonn. He was exhausted. *(Puts on tweed cap; speaks, now, as MAXIMILLIAN ZYLBERSTEIN.)* You know how many hours it takes to fly from Cairns, Australia, to Bonn, Germany? I'll tell you. A *hundred!* You know how many peanuts you eat in a hundred hours?!

ACTOR #3. Maximillian Zylberstein had the distinction of being the oldest of the new citizens to arrive under the Project Homecoming Law.

ACTOR #1. He was also the first concentration camp survivor to claim German citizenship, earlier in his life, in pre-Hitler Germany.

ACTOR #1. *(Playing SIGN-IN CENTER CLERK.)* Where were you born, Herr Zylberstein?

ZYLBERSTEIN. Here and there.

SIGN-IN CENTER CLERK. Here and there?

ZYLBERSTEIN. Here and there.

SIGN-IN CENTER CLERK. Here and there, in which country?

ZYLBERSTEIN. I can't remember.

SIGN-IN CENTER CLERK. Do you have any clue at all?

ZYLBERSTEIN. None. I've been in Australia for nearly sixty years.

SIGN-IN CENTER CLERK. Shall we put down "Australia"?

ZYLBERSTEIN. I wasn't born there. I was re-located there.

SIGN-IN CENTER CLERK. Could you have been born in Poland?

ZYLBERSTEIN. I could have been.

ACTOR #3. Zylberstein was, in fact, born in Berlin ... in a working-class neighborhood called Charlottenburg.

ACTOR #1. Zylberstein remembered his childhood, vividly. His father had been an actor in the same company in which Bertold Brecht's earliest plays were first performed.

ACTOR #3. His father, Zelly Zylberstein, was gaining popularity, in 1930, just as Hitler was gaining political power.

ACTOR #1. The Zylbersteins weren't a rich family, but, they were well-off. They had a small house, overlooking the River Spree. They were loving, educated, and sophisticated.

ACTOR #3. Zelly Zylberstein was arrested, on stage, in the midst of a comic performance as the forgetful butler in the German adaptation of a George Bernard Shaw play.

ACTOR #1. He had told his family a thousand times that what was happening to other Jews in Germany could never happen to them. They were Germans. Intellectuals. They were safe.

ZYLBERSTEIN. He was incorrect.

ACTOR #1. Hitler made a shabbily dramatic example of Zelly Zylberstein's crime against the state. The popular Jewish actor was arrested and humiliated in front of an astonished audience.

ACTOR #3. His understudy was rehearsed and ready to take over Zylberstein's role, mid-performance. And he did.

ZYLBERSTEIN. My father was taken away in handcuffs. Hitler's people in the audience were yelling "Judle! Judle!" ... "Kike! Kike!". My father way crying.

ACTOR #3. The understudy entered, stage left, as Zelly Zylberstein exited, stage right. And the show went on.

ACTOR #1. At 8:15 pm, precisely the same moment of Zelly Zylberstein's arrest, Police entered the Zylberstein family's home in Charlottenburg, and arrested Zelly Zylberstein's wife *(Drumbeat)* , daughter *(Drumbeat)*, mother *(Drumbeat)*, his dying father *(Drumbeat)*, his sister *(Drumbeat)*. Zylberstein's small son, Maxie, was not in the house.

ACTOR #2/ZYLBERSTEIN. *(To audience as NARRATOR.)* The little boy ... seven years old ... was sitting on the carpeted steps in the back of the theatre, scared, weeping, watching his father being led away by the Police ... hearing people planted in the audience by Hitler screaming "Judle! Judle!" ... *(To CLERK, as ZYLBERSTEIN.)* I can see you've had a difficult day. Let's put down "Poland". Poland is a fine place to be born.

SIGN-IN CENTER CLERK. That's ever so nice of you, Herr Zylberstein. *(Types information into computer.)* "Poland" it is. *(Looks on computer screen.)* Let's find you a place to stay. Any preferences? Would you rather live in the country, or in the city?

ZYLBERSTEIN. Berlin, please.

SIGN-IN CENTER CLERK. Berlin? Let's have a look. *(CLERK looks at computer screen.)* There is a small guest-house in the Charlottenburg district. The listing indicates they can take you for a few weeks, maybe longer, if you're willing to help out on the desk.

ZYLBERSTEIN. Yes.

SING-IN CENTER CLERK. I can put you up here in Bonn, for tonight, in a very nice hotel, just here on the market-square. You can travel to Berlin, in the morning.

ZYLBERSTEIN. I'd prefer to go to Berlin, now, if you please.

SIGN-IN CENTER CLERK. Are you sure?

ZYLBERSTEIN. Quite sure.

ACTOR #3. Within the hour, Zylberstein was driven from Bonn to Cologne, where he boarded a Lufthanza flight to Berlin.

ACTOR #1. By all that was holy, a man of Zylberstein's age should have been exhausted by his journey, but, he was not at all. In fact, Zylberstein felt more energetic than he had any time during several prior decades.

ACTOR #2. *(As NARRATOR.)* In Beersheba, Israel, Zev Golem, had a plan, as well.

ZEV GOLEM. I firmly believe that we must monitor Germany's "Project Homecoming". I and many, many others believe this project is neo-Nazi based ... designed to complete Hitler's mission: the elimination of world Jewry. Our organization must maintain the strongest possible military presence in Germany, at this time.

ACTOR #3. Zev Golem had organized a meeting of one hundred trusted Jewish militants, members of a world-wide secret Jewish army called "Jews, Forever". Among them, we meet a Czech, Rifka Borenstein, head of the Women's Committee.

(ACTOR #3 now speaks to audience as RIFKA, angry, dangerous ...)

RIFKA. If you think they do not plan to slaughter six-million *more* Jews, you are insane! They are Germans! They are *born* to kill Jews! They are *defined* by killing Jews!

ACTOR #2. May we ask Rifka Borenstein and Zev Golem what they are proposing to the Executive Committee, specifically?

ZEV GOLEM. We must organize our people in Germany, immediately!

RIFKA. I will personally go to live in Germany, as soon as possible, for this purpose.

ZEV GOLEM. As will I.

RIFKA. We're both speaking a good German, so we can stay undercover, easily.

ZEV GOLEM. We propose that we go to live in Germany as new German citizens under the Project Homecoming program.

RIFKA. Our people on the inside can deal with the necessary paperwork. I've checked everything. Zev Golem and I have already been pre-approved.

ZEV GOLEM. Once we're living there, we can organize our people, properly.

RIFKA. We must be able to disseminate news, worldwide, immediately, if and when the German begin to kill Jews, again.

ZEV GOLEM. We must be ready to strike back, militarily, as well.

RIFKA. This is our job.

ZEV GOLEM. We are the policemen of the world's Jews.

ACTOR #2. You'll have no opposition from anyone on this committee. We back you, entirely. May God be with you, as well.

ACTOR #3. *(As NARRATOR.)* And that is how Rifka Borenstein and Zev Golem came to emigrate to Germany as new Jewish citizens.

ZEV GOLEM. *(To RIFKA; urgently.)* Rifka! Pay attention! I think this fat one is our clerk! *(To SIGN-IN CLERK #2.)* My name is Allen Schwartz.

RIFKA. And I'm his wife ... Mrs. Schwartz.

(ACTOR #2 plays SIGN-IN CENTER CLERK #2.)

SIGN-IN CENTER CLERK #2. You're both American-born?

RIFKA. Yes. Both of us. But, we've been living in Israel for several years, so, our English is a little rusty.

SIGN-IN CENTER CLERK #2. Your German is not bad.

ZEV GOLEM. Thank you.

RIFKA. Thank you.

SIGN-IN CENTER CLERK #2. *(Puts rubber-stamp mark on several official citizenship-papers ...)* Fine. Fine. Fine. Fine. Fine. Your papers are in order. Welcome to Germany ... fellow citizens.

RIFKA. *Vielen Dank.*

ZEV GOLEM. *Danke.*

SIGN-IN CENTER CLERK #2. Bitte. *(SIGN-IN CENTER CLERK looks up at imagined line of people, waiting.)* Nächste?

ACTOR #3. Mike Linsky spent his first day as crew chief with a smile from ear to ear. At dinner, that night, he had nothing but praise for their new country.

MIKE LINSKY. Can you imagine? Can you imagine? Here I am, runnin' a crew of fifty men, TV cameras, everywhere ... Three container ships in a nest, waiting! Can you imagine this? Business is gettin' better and better, and everybody's givin' me the credit! *Everybody!* Herr Friedlander ... Günter ... I'm s'pose'ta call him by his first name, Günter ... He owns the docks ... He gave out this interview sayin' that he's gonna' be bringing back fifty jobs ... He's gonna' be hiring twenty-five new men ... all new citizens ... Jews! Can you imagine? ...

ACTOR #3. But, everybody in Bremerhaven wasn't as euphoric as Michael Linsky. Gustav Giesling, for example, was totally offended by Günter Friedlander's decision to hire twenty-five Jewish citizens to work the docks.

GUSTAV GIESLING. There are ten million Germans out of work! Ten million! And out of fifty new jobs, twenty-five are going to Jews? I say "No"! I say "Strike"! ... *Strike! Strike!*

ACTORS #1, #2, & #3. *Strike! Strike! Strike!*

ACTOR #3. There were five hundred union workers gathered together in the hall. Those with jobs were hesitant. *(Calls out as FISH-PACKER.)* I waited a year for my job! I don't want to strike!

GUSTAV GIESLING. You can't be so greedy! This is a union, not a rat-race! We must protect our brothers and sisters who are out of work, as well as those who are working. Strike! Strike!

ACTORS #1, #2, & #3. *Strike! Strike! Strike!*

ACTOR #3. Götz Burger spoke, briefly, but convincingly.

GÖTZ BURGER. My name is Götz Burger. Many of you know me from the docks. I have been demoted as crew chief, so that a Jew can take my place! So that a Jew could be put in the spotlight! A Jew has taken my job from me. Soon, Jews will have everybody's jobs! That is our government's plan! That is why we must strike!

ACTOR #3. And, one by one, the workers were frightened or shamed into joining together ...

ACTOR #1. *(Steps d/s, to audience, as NARRATOR ...)* Heroes and villians alike are too often born of hopelessness and humiliation.

ACTOR #2. In Berlin, a cable-television installer named Allen Schwartz got an urgent message to return a call from his wife at her office.

(Lights shift to ... ZEV GOLEM, as if talking on telephone.)

ZEV GOLEM. I need to speak with Mrs. Schwartz. This is her husband.

RIFKA. *(As if on telephone.)* Hello?

ZEV GOLEM. It's Zev, Rifka. Issak said it was urgent.

RIFKA. We must meet, immediately, Zev. There's trouble.

ACTOR #1. Zev Golem went to Bremenhaven, immediately, along with Rifka and sixteen other "new citizens", all members of the rapidly-growing underground army, "Jews, Forever".

ZEV GOLEM. Are you Herr Linsky?

MIKE LINSKY. I am, yuh.

ZEV GOLEM. I'm Allen Schwartz. I'm assigned to your crew.

MIKE LINSKY. Hey, that's great. *(They shake hands.)* Call me "Mike", Al, okay?

ZEV GOLEM. Fine ... Mike.

MIKE LINSKY. You speak English, huh?

ZEV GOLEM. I do, yes, Mike.

MIKE LINSKY. How come?

ZEV GOLEM. I speak many languages, Mike.

MIKE LINSKY. Have you worked on the water at all?

ZEV GOLEM. Excuse me?

MIKE LINSKY. Hey, no problem. You speak any German?

ZEV GOLEM. I speak German.

MIKE LINSKY. Great! I'm gonna' put you with Hans on that first container-ship. We're a little short-handed, today. We've got some union problems. Nothin' serious. The boss is workin' on it.

ACTOR #3. Mike Linsky's assessment of the situation as "nothing serious" was greatly and absurdly hopeful, given the fact that Gustav Giesling, Götz Burger, and several other union men were now carrying guns.

GUSTAV GIESLING. *(Brandishing pistol, discreetly.)* Under no circumstances do our guns come out unless *their* guns come out! ... Is that clear?

ACTOR #1. Clear, Herr Giesling.

ACTOR #3. Clear, Herr Giesling.

ACTOR #1. Absolutely clear, Herr Giesling.

ACTOR #3. Each morning, at 5 a.m., Maximillian Zylberstein woke, and left his warm bed at number 25 Hardenbergstraße, and walked six blocks to stop and stare at number 16 Tribestraße, a small one-family house overlooking a tiny tributary of the river Spree, and a large park, Charlottenburg Schlosspark, beyond. Zylberstein had spent his boyhood in this house, until his father was arrested. This morning, Zylberstein walked for nearly 40 minutes along Otto-Shur-Allee, to an undistinguished 4-story apartment house at 12 Frederickstraße. This is where little Maxie Zylberstein lived when *he* was arrested and, subsequently, sent to Buchenwald. He opened the front door and he went inside. He climbed the steps to the 3rd floor and he knocked on the door. A 65-year-old woman answered. Her name was Esla Krebs.

(ACTOR #3 now talks to ZYLBERSTEIN as ESLA KREBS.)

ZYLBERSTEIN. Max Zylberstein.

ESLA KREBS. You're much older than I thought you'd be. You must be nearly my mother's age.

ZYLBERSTEIN. Fifteen years younger. I'm very healthy.

ESLA KREBS. I'm glad to hear it. Truthfully, there's very little to do, other than to look in on her, from time to time. And, of course, to call me, if there's a reason.

ZYLBERSTEIN. I see you have a piano.

ESLA KREBS. We have many pianos. Two in the apartment, here, and several in storage. My mother taught piano to children for years and years. She had her own school ... just two streets away ... the

Charlottenburg Kinder-Flügel. It was quite well-known. When I was growing up, in this very apartment, there was always beautiful music in the air. Bach, Beethoven, Brahms. Do you play the piano?

ZYLBERSTEIN. I did ... a bit ... when I was a child.

ESLA KREBS. Where did you grow up?

ZYLBERSTEIN. Here and there.

ESLA KREBS. Here and there?

ZYLBERSTEIN. Here and there.

ESLA KREBS. I'll have to get to work, soon. It's terrible, our job-situation in Germany, just now. I've had to take a job nearly two hours from here.

ZYLBERSTEIN. So you told me on the telephone.

ESLA KREBS. It's terrible. Still and all, it's better to work than to not work.

ZYLBERSTEIN. Much.

ESLA KREBS. It's a matter of dignity, don't you think?

ZYLBERSTEIN. I do think dignity matters, greatly, Frau Krebs.

ESLA KREBS. Let me take you in to mother's room. *(ESLA KREBS moves upstage, as if leading ZYLBERSTEIN into her mother's bedroom, where ACTOR #1 sits swarthed in lacey sheets and blankets, as UTA KREBS.)* She's just there. She won't talk to you, at all. She can't do much more than just lie there. She can hum, a bit. She does that from time to time. If she weeps, don't worry yourself. There's nothing can be done. You want to listen that she's still breathing ... or for anything, you know, quite unusual. Call me, immediately, if something quite unusual, you know ...

ZYLBERSTEIN. *(Completes her thought ...)* ... Happens? ...

ESLA KREBS. *(Smiles)* Happens.

ZYLBERSTEIN. I assure you I will.

ESLA KREBS. I rest assured. Let me show you the kitchen and the bathroom. Oh, yes, this is the nasty part of your job.

ZYLBERSTEIN. Cleaning her.

ESLA KREBS. Changing her bag. She has a bag attached.

ZYLBERSTEIN. It won't be a problem.

ESLA KREBS. *(Replaces plastic bag filled with sawdust with fresh plastic bag.)* You've seen them before?

ZYLBERSTEIN. I've seen everything you could possibly imagine in life that anyone might call "nasty".

ESLA KREBS. Oh, dear! ... That's life, I suppose.

ZYLBERSTEIN. Yes, Fray Krebs. I suppose that is life.

ESLA KREBS. Well, then, good luck. There's plenty of food in the fridge ... Take whatever you want. The TV is ordinary. The books are for reading. Whatever is here is yours to use. Feel free.

ZYLBERSTEIN. Oh, I do, thank you.

ESLA KREBS. Well. I'll be off, then. I'll call you in a while to see if everything's all right.

ZYLBERSTEIN. You can rely on me, Frau Krebs.

ESLA KREBS. I'm sure I can, Herr Zylberstein. You seem a most reliable man.

(Changes voice, again, to NARRATOR: speaks to audience.)

ACTOR #3. And Esla Krebs went off to work, two hours away, relieved to have found anyone at all willing to sit and watch her mother, Uta Krebs ... 94, feeble, and failing.

ACTOR #1. Maximillion Zylberstein stood staring at Uta Krebs for a full two hours, without moving or talking, until he realized that he had to urinate. Saying nothing, he peed on Uta's bedroom floor.

(ZYLBERSTEIN mimes urinating on the floor. ACTOR #3 enters carrying squeeze-bottle of water, from which she drips water on to floor in front of UTA KREBS ...)

ACTOR #3. And then, once he'd relieved himself of his urine, he began talking to Uta Krebs, quietly, thoughtfully, relieving himself of thoughts he'd kept hidden within for years and years. At first, Zylberstein's voice was like a child's ...

ZYLBERSTEIN. Hello, it's me, Frau Krebs ... Maxie Zylberstein ... from upstairs. I've come down for my lesson. *(ZYLBERSTEIN plays a child's two-handed exercise on toy piano.)* It was my left hand that bothered you, wasn't it, Frau Krebs? You always called my left hand "lazy", yes? ... *(ZYLBERSTEIN continues to play the piece, lightly, talking to UTA, underscoring his words ...)* It is an amazing thing what the brain chooses to shlep through this life, isn't it? I mean, it just *amazes* me what I've been stuck having to remember. *(Beat)* I remember your breasts ... your nipples, especially. You were feeding your daughter during my piano lesson. You couldn't have been more than twenty-five. I was eleven. You know, I expected to show up here, this morning, and have your daughter look like you. I was ready to be shocked by the similarity. But, she's nearly three times the age you were when I last saw you, isn't she? I mean, she looks more like your *grandmother* looked than like you looked, doesn't she? *(Beat)* Your breasts were full and white, crisscrossed with blue veins. Your nipples were enormous. *(Beat)* You caught me looking and you liked it. "Want a drink, little man?" you asked me. You were always smiling with a kind of sexy smile. *(Beat)* In fact, I was weeping. I didn't know, at the time, why seeing your milky breasts and nipples made me so sad, Frau Krebs, but, I know now. *(Beat)* I don't think you knew my mother, did you? Tante Elke wasn't really my tante. She was my father's cousin, I think. I don't think you ever met my mother. My mother's breasts were enormous. I can still smell them. Imagine! Almost eighty years later, and I can still smell them. *(Beat)* Sometimes, I go for a long time without bathing, so I can have the same smell on my own body. *(Beat)* It was so nice of Tante Elke to take me in, wasn't it? She was so kind to me. She never tried to be my mother, not once. She used to say it to me, just like that: "I'm not your mother, Maxie. I'll never be your mother. Your mother was an angel." *(Beat)* So was Tante Elke, Frau Krebs. She took me in to her family like I was one of her own. She held me in her arms at night until I fell asleep. And sometimes, when I'd have the dream and wake up crying, she'd already be at my bed ... As if she knew I was having the dream, and she'd come to my bed, to be ready for me when I woke up, crying. *(Beat)* I found a cure for my bad dreams, Frau Krebs. I never sleep. If you don't sleep, you can't dream ... You can't wake up, so frightened. *(Beat)* Tante Elke said you called the police and turned us in, because you were jealous of our clothes. Tante Elke made the most beautiful clothes for us. *(Beat)* Tante Elke said we should forgive you for calling the police. Tante Elke said there was no good in hating people. It was like a poison, to hate people. That's what my Tante Elke tried to teach me, the same way you tried to teach me to play this piano. Both of you failed! ... *(Beat)* They killed Tante Elke and all of her children. I was saved because Major Daniel Reitz saw my father play in an Ernst Toller play, three times. My father made him laugh, three times, so, he let his son live. *(Beat)* For the last seventy years or so, I thought I would find you, one day, and kill you,

Frau Krebs. It was a kind of pleasant day-dream for me to imagine you, just there, and me, just here, able to kill you, so easily. *(Beat)* I won't kill you, Frau Krebs. I'll come here, every day, and I'll tell you everything that I remember, And you'll listen. I know you can hear me, Uta. I'm sure of it.

(He plays his piano-piece, again, as ESLA KREBS re-enter.)

ESLA KREBS. You're playing the piano?
ZYLBERSTEIN. Yes, I've played for her, most of the day.
ESLA KREBS. Oh, lucky mother!
ZYLBERSTEIN. She ate very little.
ESLA KREBS. She would starve to death if I let her.
ZYLBERSTEIN. You mustn't let her!
ESLA KREBS. Oh, I won't! *(Sees wetness on floor.)* It's wet.
ZYLBERSTEIN. I'm afraid she had an accident.
ESLA KREBS. I'll clean it up.
ZYLBERSTEIN. You don't mind?
ESLA KREBS. I don't mind at all. *(She gets rag, wipes up puddle of urine from floor.)* You didn't mind being here?
ZYLBERSTEIN. I didn't mind at all. I enjoyed talking with your mother.
ESLA KREBS. You did?
ZYLBERSTEIN. I did indeed.
ESLA KREBS. Did she respond at all?
ZYLBERSTEIN. I think she did.
ESLA KREBS. Lucky mother! *(To Imagined Mother on imagined bed.)* We're so lucky to have Herr Zylberstein with us, aren't we, Mother? *(We hear ... a woman's moan from ACTOR #1.)* Are you speaking, Mother? *(To ZYLBERSTEIN.)* I think she's trying to thank you.
ZYLBERSTEIN. She probably is.
ESLA KREBS. Lucky mother! So, you'll come back, tomorrow?
ZYLBERSTEIN. Tomorrow and every day. It's my pleasure.
ESLA KREBS. I'm so pleased, Herr Zylberstein.
ZYLBERSTEIN. I'm so pleased to have pleased you, Frau Krebs.
ESLA KREBS. This is so special for my mother.

ACTOR #1. And with a great gentlemanly flourish, Zylberstein took Esla Kreb's hand in his, bowed ...

ESLA KREBS. ... Und *kissed* it! *(To audience, as ACTOR #3.)* Esla Krebs was shocked, but she allowed her hand to linger in the old man's hand for a full minute. It was more affection than Esla Krebs had felt in years.

(ACTOR #2 steps into spotlight ...)

ACTOR #2. Sam Linsky and Anna Giesling were negotiating a kiss of their own. They were on bikes, on their way to a school picnic. The route to the picnic was somewhat circuitous. They stopped on a small, brown-sandy beach, on the edge of the harbor, directly opposite Mike Linsky's dock.

(Lights shift to ... ANNA and SAM.)

ANNA. Shall we park our bikes for a while?

SAM. Are you tired?

ANNA. No ... yes. A bit.

SAM. Fine. If you're tired, we should stop.

ACTOR #2. Anna and Sam held hands, timidly. They both knew that they were about to make love for the first time in their lives, in the paper-white light of the glistening spring sunshine, on the banks of Anna's beloved River Weser.

ANNA. I love the River Weser. I look at it every day of my life. I can't imagine spending a day, alive, and not.

SAM. That's like me, back home in Gloucester. I walked on Good Harbor Beach, every day, no matter what.

ANNA. You miss Gloucester, a lot, don't you?

SAM. I guess. Mostly at night.

ANNA. I'd love to see Gloucester.

SAM. I'd love you to. Someday, maybe I could take you there.

ANNA. I'd love to, so much!

ACTOR #2. Without a word, they lay down on the sand, side by side, knowing that they would both remember this day, vividly, for the rest of their lives. Neither hurried the event.

SAM. *(To ANNA.)* Good Harbor Beach is awesome. There's this brook at one end that goes under this wooden footbridge. When the tide's goin' out, you can ride the current. It's fantastic!

ANNA. *Wie ist der Strand ...* What's the beach like? *Sandig, steinig, felsig? ...*

SAM. Oh, right! *Strand* is beach.

ANNA. *Sandig? ...*

SAM. Sandy.

ANNA. Right.

SAM. Good Harbor beach is totally *sandig.* It's all really soft, white *sandig.* It's beautiful. So are you.

ANNA. *Kahn man hier ohne Gefar schwimmen?*

SAM. "Schwimmin" has got to mean "swimming", right?

ANNA. Right. Kann man hier ohne Gefar ... Is it safe for ...

SAM. *Schwimmin*! Good Harbor Beach is definitely safe for *schwimmen.*

ANNA. *Ist dort ungefährlich für Kinder?*

SAM. What's *"ungefährlich"*?

ANNA. "Safe".

SAM. Oh, yuh. Totally *ungefährlich für Kinder.* I started *schwimmin* there, alone, when I was just a little Kinder.

ANNA. *Gibt es gefährliche Strömungen?*

SAM. Wait! Wait! If "ungefährlich" means "safe", then does "gefährlich" means "dangerous"?

ANNA. You're so clever!

SAM. Selma said that, too.

ANNA. I hope I meet Selma.

ACTOR #2. And then, Sam told Anna a small, sad bit of truth.

SAM. Grandma Selma's not real crazy about Germans. She had German and Polish cousins that got killed by the Nazis.

ANNA. That's terrible. Why?

SAM. They were Jewish. I'm Jewish. Remember?

ANNA. I forgot. I forgot that. It's nothing to me that you're Jewish.

SAM. It's nothing to my father, too, but, it's not nothing to me. *(Beat)* My Grandfather Nathan was really religious. He died, two years ago. Grandpa Nathan was my best friend ... before you.

ANNA. You always say such nice things to me! ... I wish I knew your grandfather.

SAM. Me, too. I guess you do, kinda'. There's a lot of him in me. At least, that's what Grandma Selma's always sayin'. Grandpa Nathan was the reason I got Bar Mitzvahed ... That's when a Jewish boy becomes a man ... a Jewish man, like, officially. My father didn't really want to get me Bar Mitzvahed, and my mother isn't Jewish, so, she didn't care, either way. But, my Grandpa Nathan, he insisted. Grandpa Nathan told me there have got to be Jews on earth, no matter what, and I totally agree. When I have children, I really hope they study Hebrew and get Bar Mitzvahed.

ANNA. I would never object.

SAM. Really?

ANNA. Really. I think it's important to have religion in a family. We're not at all religious in my house, not like some of my friends are, and I'm always jealous of them. Having my children be Jewish would be fine.

SAM. It would?

ANNA. Sure. Why not? I never met a Jewish person before I met you. From things my father said, I thought you might be very different from what you are.

SAM. What am I?

ANNA. Everything I admire. Except for your Deutsch. You didn't finish your sentence in Deutsch.

SAM. I know. There was a word at the end ...

ANNA. *Strömungen* ... It means strong waters ... current.

SAM. Oh, right. There's a little island that's just off the beach, where the water gets wick'id rough. There's this cross-*Strömungen* that gets ya', if you're not careful. *(Without warning.)* If you weren't here for me, I would've been *schwimmen* home, already ... *ungefährlich*, or not.

ANNA. I'm glad you feel that way.

SAM. What did your father say about me?

ANNA. My father doesn't know you. If he knew you, he would admire you the way I do.

ACTOR #2. Anna changed the subject, abruptly, moving from The Preliminaries to The Main Event.

ANNA. Can we do some kissing, now?

SAM. Is that like a German thing? ... Girls asking for the kissing?

ANNA. Oh, is it wrong for me to do the asking?

SAM. No, no, no! I'm just really nervous about the kissing going further. I mean, I *want* it to go further, but, I don't wanna' mess things up between us. I mean, I'm frightened that if I lose you, I won't have *anything*.

ANNA. You won't lose me.

SAM. I'm really glad to know this. You won't lose me, either, Anna. No chance.

ANNA. Can we do the kissing?

SAM. You're really into the kissing, huh?

ANNA. I've never met anybody I've wanted to do the kissing with so much, before you.

SAM. Oh, my God. That is like such a fantastically beautiful thing you just said. *(Beat)* Anna, this is the first time in my whole life that I ever kissed anybody I was in love with.

ANNA. *Mein Gott!*

SAM. What?

ANNA. That is such a fantastically beautiful thing you just said.

(They kiss.)

ACTOR #2. Sam and Anna snuck away, together, almost every afternoon for the next three weeks, to the same small, secluded beach, for secret kissing-sessions, with occasional breaks for language lessons exchanged in German and in English. Anna taught Sammy her favorite poem, a verse from a sonnet by Rilke.

(SAM and ANNA lie on their stomachs on the inclined ramp – their "beach" – side by side.)

SAM. *Und fast ein Mädchen wars und ging hervor ...*

ANNA. She was nearly a woman ...

SAM. *Aus diesem einigen Glück von Sang und Leir ...*

ANNA. She sprang forth from a beautiful song and the sound of a lyre ...

SAM. *Und glänzte klar durch ihre Frühlingsschleir ...*

ANNA. Shining through clear veils of Springtime ...

SAM. *Und machte sich ein Bette in meinem Ohr.*

ANNA. She made a bed for herself in my ear.

SAM. *Und schlief in mir.*

ANNA. And she slept inside me.

ACTOR #1. *(To audience, as NARRATOR.)* Sammy never told ANNA how sad he was, how much he missed his beloved Gloucester, Massachusetts ... his school-friends ... his English language.

ACTOR #3. *(To audience, as NARRATOR.)* And Anna never told Sammy how her father raged at the dining table, every night, railing against Germany's new Jewish citizens.

ACTOR #1. Gustav Giesling promised to help cleanse Germany of what he called its "disgusting blight".

ACTOR #3. Anna knew enough to say nothing. Not a word.

ACTOR #2. The situation on the docks at Bremerhaven worsened, each day.

ACTOR #1. Inspired by Mike Linsky's well-publicized success, Jewish laborers began to arrive in Germany looking for work, many looking for Linsky, himself, who had become a kind of symbol of Project Homecoming's promise.

ACTOR #3. Linsky was now overall boss of three active docks, second only to Günter Friedlander, himself.

ACTOR #2. Thus, a fair number of Jewish laborers ... more than a thousand new citizens, in all ... came directly to Bremerhaven, to live and to work.

ACTOR #1. Any new citizen who was ready to do an honest day's labor found a job waiting on Mike Linsky's dock, even though it almost always meant displacing an existing German worker.

(ACTOR #2, as MIKE LINSKY, talks to audience, as if talking to Crew Chiefs.)

MIKE LINSKY. I've called this meeting of crew chiefs because I want each of you to make sure the guys we're layin' off in each of your crews know that their lay-off is only temporary. We've gotta' get the new citizens on the books, right away. This we know. Chancellor Stroiber is watching us, personally. But, as soon as things settle down, I'm positive there's gonna' be work enough for everybody, and the guys we've laid off will have first crack! Herr Friedlander definitely back me up on this.

ACTOR #3. *(To audience, as NARRATOR.)* Was Mike Linsky really as trusting and as innocent as he seemed? A week before the event that the good people of Bremerhaven would come to call "The Dock 6 Catastrophe", over an evening meal of roast chicken and parsleyed potatoes, with Sammy off with a school-friend named Anna, getting what he called "a one-on-one German lesson", Mike Linsky spoke his thoughts to his wife.

(ACTOR #3 speaks to MIKE; as LIZZIE ...)

LIZZIE LINSKY. More potatoes?
MIKE LINSKY. Yuh, thanks.

(LIZ serves potatoes to MIKE, who eats, and speaks his mind to his wife, thoughtfully ...)

MIKE LINSKY. I dunno, Liz ... I think I'm changing. I used'ta think: if the world says it doesn't like Jews, okay, then, fine, I'm not gonna' be a Jew! ... When I was in 4th grade, walking home, these kids from St. Ann's Sister School jumped out from behind this big bush and they grabbed me; yelling "You Jews killed Jesus! You Jews killed Jesus!" It was like a joke. I yell back "That was two thousand years ago!" and they go "Yuh, but, we just heard about it!" ... They muckled me. Eight of 'em. I didn't wanna' advertise I was Jewish, too much, after that. You see what I'm sayin'? *(Beat. Following speech builds in its passion ...)* But, I'll tell ya' the honest-ta'-God truth, Lizzie: I think it's the kids from Saint Ann's, Hitler, and the Germans that are finally gonna make me more stand-up. I spent too much time, when I was a kid, listenin' to my mother and my grandmother talkin' horror-stories about Germans and Jew-haters. You see what I'm sayin' on this? I don't know about "retribution". That's a fancy word. What I feel in my heart is simple: Germans owe us, big time, and I got no problem takin' a job from any one of them, or givin' a job to any New Citizen that comes on to my dock lookin' for an honest day's work. What's goin' on here is just about bringin' us back to scratch! *(Embarrassed by his emotion ...)* Hey, what do I know, huh?! ... Pass me some more roast Hühnchen., huh? It's *delicious!*

ACTOR #1. The ship-building industry in Bremerhaven, once powerful and prosperous, had been all but invisible for nearly ten years.

ACTOR #3. To the shock and amazement of out-of-work ship-builders, Chancellor Rudolph Stroiber announced the re-opening of Bremerhaven's largest shipyard. *(New voice ... official, ominous.)* Ladies and gentlemen, the Chancellor of the German Republic, Rudolph Stroiber! ...

(On tape ... applause and cheers.)

RUDOLPH STROIBER. *(Wears his "official" portrait ...)* It is our intention that the Bremerhaven shipyard will be manned entirely by our new citizens. Work on a fleet of life-boats will begin, immediately.

ACTOR #3. And now, the good citizens of Bremerhaven were stunned.

ACTOR #1. Gustav Giesling and Götz Burger found support in every corner of Bremerhaven. Five hundred of Bremerhaven's unemployed workers marched to the docks to protest the first day of ship-building.

ACTOR #2. Many of these angry people carried guns and knives.

ACTOR #3. The re-opened shipyard was located just opposite Mike Linsky's dock.

GUSTAV GIESLING. *(Making a speech to the assembled workers.)* We mustn't back down! We will teach these Jews the lesson they should have learned sixty years ago!

(On tape ... sounds of an angry mob.)

ACTOR #3. They allowed Giesling to fire the first shot ...

(GIESLING fires his pistol ...)
ACTOR #3. And then, they shot him dead with a volley of more than three hundred bullets.

(Drum beats, or hammer-strokes on wood, like gunshots ... A loud

*barrage. GIESLING flies upstage, heaving and bobbing with
every bullet that passes into and through his body.)*

ACTOR #1. The angry mob stopped, dead in their tracks, stunned
by Giesling's bloody death ... and by the seventy guns now pointed at
their faces.

ACTOR #3. Rifka Borenstein made the announcement ... *(As
RIFKA, she screams, madly ...)* We've killed your leader and we will
kill any man, woman or child who shows us a gun, a knife, or even an
angry word! Go back to your houses and we will let you live. The
victim-Jews of the past are dead! We are the new Jews of the world,
and if you threaten us, we will kill you, without a moment's hesitation!

ACTOR #1. Every man and woman in the angry mob heard
Rifka's words.

ACTOR #3. They turned from the shipyard and they went to their
homes.

ACTOR #2. Gustav Giesling lay dead. And just across the river
from the dock, on a tiny, brown-sandy beach, on the edge of River
Weser, Anna Giesling lay dead, as well ... *(Lights fade up on ... ANNA
and SAMMY, locked in a kiss.)* While she and Sammy lay together,
making love, Anna's life was stopped by a single bullet, gone astray,
as bullets are wont do, into the hearts and heads of the innocent ...
Perhaps it was a bullet intended for Gustav Giesling? Perhaps, it was a
bullet from Giesling's own gun? ... We'll never know.

(Suddenly, a final gunshot. ANNA flinches, moans ...)

ANNA. *Uggghhhhhhhh.*
SAM. Anna? What's happening? ... Anna? ...

(ACTOR #2 walks to ANNA, places a red silk square on her breast.)

ACTOR #2. When Sammy turned Anna's limp body over, there
was a flooding river of blood on her dress, just above her breast.

SAM. *ANNNNNNNAAAAAAAA!*

ACTOR #2. Anna Giesling's funeral captured the imaginations of
the people of the world. Her death was compared to the death of
another young Anna ...

ACTOR #1. Anne Franck.

ACTOR #3. And, once again, the same agonized words were heard, whispered by mourners through their tears ...

ACTOR #2. *Tragisch.*

ACTOR #1. ... *Une tragedie* ...

ACTOR #3. Tragic.

ACTOR #2. *Unbrauchbar.*

ACTOR #1. ... *Inutile* ...

ACTOR #3. A useless waste.

ACTOR #2. *Undenkbar.*

ACTOR #1. ... *Impensable* ...

ACTOR #3. Unthinkable.

ACTOR #1. Sammy spoke at Anna's funeral, invoking the words of the German poet, Rainer Maria Rilke, from his delicate "Sonnet to Orpheus" ...

(He now speaks as SAMMY, directly to audience. He is weeping.)

SAM. *Aus diesem einigen Glück von Sang und Leir* ...

ANNA. She sprang forth from the beautiful song and the sound of a lyre ...

SAM. *Und glänzte klar durch ihre Frühlingsschleir* ...

ANNA. Shining through clear veils of Springtime ...

SAM. *Und machte sich ein Bette in meinem Ohr.*

ANNA. She made a bed for herself in my ear.

SAM. *Und schlief in mir.*

ANNA. And she will sleep inside me ...

SAM. ... Forever and ever.

ACTOR. Anna Giesling's ashes were scattered on the River Weser. Sammy moved back to Gloucester, within the month, to live with his grandmother, who had never doubted for an instant that something terrible would happen, if her son Michael moved his family to Germany.

ACTOR #3. Liz and Mike Linsky stayed married for ten more years, before their marriage dissolved, and Liz moved back to Massachusetts to live near her family and friends.

ACTOR #2. Mike re-married, five years later. His new wife was German-Jewish, a New Citizen.

ACTOR #3. In Hamburg, Pierre Chambray and Jacques Burstin lived together in their tiny, chic apartment above their flower-shop ...

ACTOR #1. Married ...

ACTOR #2. They stayed faithful to each other, loyal and loving till the end of their lives.

ACTOR #3. And in Berlin, a full year after Maximillian Zylberstein first began daily visits to Uta Krebs, Uta breathed her last.

ACTOR #2. After Uta's death, Zylberstein saw little reason to continue, and he died, as well.

ACTOR #3. Esla Krebs buried Maximillian Zylberstein next to her mother.

ACTOR #2. They stayed together, side by side, into eternity.

ACTOR #3. And in Berlin, a few months after Rudolph Stroiber's death, after more than fifty failed attempts, the German government unveiled its first-ever monument honoring the Jewish dead.

ACTOR #2. And now, facing the 21st-Century, Germany tries to lead Europe into unification ... for economic power, for living space ...

ACTORS #1, #2 & #3. *Lebensraum.*

(Music in ...)

ACTOR #1. This play is fantasy. Nothing you've seen tonight ever happened. Everything was imagined. Everything was Art.

ACTOR #3. Art has no answers, no solutions, or resolutions ...

ACTOR #1. Art has only vision and revision ...

ACTOR #2. Art has only hope and more hope ... again and again, against circumstance and history ...

ACTOR #1. What we hope life might be, again and again, against what we see it has been.

ACTOR #3. In hope, there is a reason to continue.

ACTOR #1. This play was written with a special love for Jews and for Germans. History is written and cannot be changed. But, the Future is *being* written by us ... now. It is a time to understand what has passed, to join hands, and to move forward, to forgive, and to never forget.

ACTOR #3. To forgive ...

ACTOR #2. *(As ZYLBERSTEIN ...)* Tante Elke said we should

forgive you. Tante Elke said there's no good in hating people. It's like a poison, to hate people.

ACTOR #1. To never forget ...

ACTOR #3. *(As RIFKA ...)* The victim-Jews of the past are dead! We are the new Jews of the world, and if you threaten us, we will kill you, without a moment's hesitation!

ACTOR #1. To never forget ...

ACTOR #2. *(As ZYLBERSTEIN ...)* I'll come here, every day, and I'll tell you everything that I remember. And you'll listen. *(Looks directly at audience, speaks clearly, seriously ...)* I know you can hear me. I'm sure of it. *(He smiles; speaks with his own friendly voice, again, as NARRATOR, directly to audience ...)* The lights begin to fade ... We Actors step forward for our bows, and think about food and rest, and tomorrow night's performance of our play.

ACTOR #1. But, in Germany, in a river-port called Bremenhaven, Jews and Germans join hands, and, together, speak the words "Nimmer wieder" – never again – over and over ...

(The THREE ACTORS will now move forward and drop pieces of their various costumes on to a pile, down-stage center. They will speak in the various voices of the characters they are releasing ...)

ACTOR #2. *(As GIESLING.)* Nimmer wieder.
ACTOR #3. *(As LIZZIE LINSKY.)* Never again.
ACTOR #2. *(As MIKE LINSKY.)* Never again.
ACTOR #3. *(As RIFKA.)* Never again.
ACTOR #1. *(As SAMMY.)* Nimmer wieder.
ACTOR #3. *(As ANNA.)* Never again.
ACTOR #2. *(As ZYLBERSTEIN.)* Never again.

(The THREE ACTORS now stand in a line, facing front.)

ACTOR #3. *(Simply ...)* The play is over.

(The lights fade out.)

Property Plot

Various portraits with head and hands cut off
Briefcase
Microphones
Tomato
White plastic sheet
Rubber fish
Basketball
Smoking pipe
Bucket
Flash paper
Letter in envelope
Small toy limousine
Coffee pot
2 coffee mugs
Pistol
Bed sheets and blankets
Plastic bag filled with sawdust
Empty plastic bag
Squeeze bottle of water
Toy piano (functional)
Guns
Drums
Coat racks
Hammer and wood block

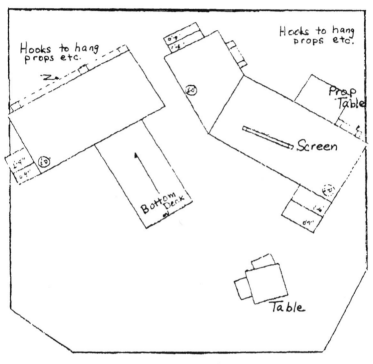

SET DESIGN
for Gloucester Stage Production and
Miranda Theatre, NYC, Production
by Lisa Pegnato

CPSIA information can be obtained
at www.ICGtesting.com
Printed in the USA
BVHW040948051021
618192BV00017B/653